# FAKING IT
# FOR THE CAMERAS

## JUSTINE LEWIS

**Harlequin® ROMANCE**

Recycling programs for this product may not exist in your area.

ISBN-13: 978-1-335-47093-5

Faking It for the Cameras

Harlequin Enterprises ULC
22 Adelaide St. West, 41st Floor
Toronto, Ontario M5H 4E3, Canada
www.Harlequin.com

HarperCollins Publishers
Macken House, 39/40 Mayor Street Upper,
Dublin 1, D01 C9W8, Ireland
www.HarperCollins.com

**Printed in U.S.A.**

1 2 3 4 5 6 7 8 9 10 HDC 28 27 26 25

**Passport to Paradise**

*Final destination: happily-ever-after!*

The heat is rising, adventure is calling...
So why not strap in and get swept away to the
world's most luxurious locations? Lands of white sands,
blue skies—and sizzling nights...

Follow our intrepid travelers as they check their
baggage and lose themselves in first-class romance. But
are their connections just for the summer...or are these
jet-setters en route to their five-star forever afters?

Grab your ticket for...

*Marriage Ruse in Paradise* by Susan Meier

*Hired for One Tuscan Summer* by Jessica Gilmore

*Faking It for the Cameras* by Justine Lewis

*Surprise Reunion in Croatia* by Ella Hayes

*One Bed Between Rivals* by Joss Wood

Available now!

*Her Big Fake Greek Wedding Date* by Michele Renae

Coming next month!

Dear Reader,

Oh, I loved writing this book—Cinderella and fake relationships are two tropes you can have so much fun with, and I did. But still, characters will sometimes take over, and the book turned more angsty and serious as I went on.

Gracie is happy in her life; it might not be exciting, but it's meaningful to her. There are tragedies in her past that she just doesn't want to poke but tries to leave well alone.

Gorgeous Connor is at a crossroads in his life—but the one thing he knows he needs is Gracie. He just doesn't know yet how much.

I hope you enjoy Connor and Gracie's story—dive in!

*Justine*

xx

P.S. A "rashie" is a lightweight T-shirt (long or short sleeves) that is worn over swimsuits in Australia to protect your skin from the sun (aka a rash guard or a rash vest). They are commonplace here, with children and adults. They are important sun protection but not usually flattering. Particularly fluorescent yellow ones.

**Justine Lewis** writes uplifting, heartwarming contemporary romances. She lives in Australia with her hero husband, two teenagers and an outgoing puppy. When she isn't writing, she loves to walk her dog in the bush near her house, attempt to keep her garden alive and search for the perfect frock. She loves hearing from readers, and you can visit her at justinelewis.com.

**Books by Justine Lewis**

**Harlequin Romance**

***If the Fairy Tale Fits...***

*Beauty and the Playboy Prince*

***Invitation from Bali***

*Breaking the Best Friend Rule*
*The Billionaire's Plus-One Deal*

***Princesses' Night Out***

*How to Win Back a Royal*

***Summer Escapes***

*Dating Game with Her Enemy*

***Cinderellas in Seville***

*CEO's Spanish Fling*

*Fiji Escape with Her Boss*
*Back in the Greek Tycoon's World*
*Swipe Right for Mr. Perfect*
*Italian Tycoon to Remember*

Visit the Author Profile page at Harlequin.com.

For my Dad

Who taught me how to swim in the ocean

# CHAPTER ONE

Gracie Sutherland sat across the desk from her boss and best friend, Virginia, in Virginia's office a storey above the pools where Gracie taught swimming lessons. The smell of chlorine pervaded the entire building, even up into Virginia's office. Despite knowing Virginia for a decade and a half, Gracie had never seen her look quite like this. Virginia was trying so hard not to smile that her entire face was contorted.

'What's the matter?' Gracie asked.

'We've had an interesting request for some private lessons.'

This wasn't unusual. Virginia's swim school, White Horses, offered private lessons, even at private pools. This didn't explain the way Virginia's mouth was twitching.

'A very lucrative request,' Virginia continued.

This *was* unusual. It was important to Virginia, as it was to Gracie, that anyone who wanted to learn could regardless of their means. Virginia charged students as little as possible, which meant that over the years, she had come close to not being able to pay her mortgage on several occasions. The pools also needed upgrades that she could hardly afford.

'I'd like you to do it,' Virginia said.

'Of course.'

'Maybe listen to what it involves first.'

'They want swimming lessons?'

'Yes. It's an adult.'

White Horses taught people of all ages. And adults typically wanted to do their lessons in private, usually scheduling them first thing in the morning or at night.

'He's thirty-five.'

Gracie nodded. A couple of years older than her. And hardly the oldest student she'd ever had. Gracie had taught several people in their sixties. Swimming was great exercise, placing less strain on joints. 'Does he have any special needs I should know about?'

'No underlying conditions, as far as I know. He's quite healthy, very fit by all accounts.'

Teaching a fit person would be easier than teaching someone with a condition that needed managing. Gracie had special skills in teaching people with injuries or illness to learn to swim, as swimming could be excellent therapy. She didn't understand what the fuss was about.

'That's all you want to know?' her friend pressed.

'Does he want to do the lessons here at the pool?'

'No, he's visiting from the US. He's staying out at Watsons Bay and would like to learn out there.'

'That's a bit of a pain.' Watsons Bay was in Sydney's exclusive eastern suburbs, where the easternmost tip of Sydney Harbour met the Pacific Ocean. At least an hour's drive away from Gracie's home in the southern suburbs. 'Do you know how big the pool is?'

'Fifteen metres.'

That was massive for a private pool. But still, if this man wanted to become proficient over any distance, they'd need to visit one larger than that.

Virginia pulled her funny face again. 'He needs to learn for his job.'

'What's his job?'

Virginia finally admitted defeat and smiled broadly as she delivered the next piece of news.

'He's an actor. He needs to learn for his new role. He can't swim at all, apparently.'

'Oh.' That was out of left field. But Gracie still said, 'Okay.'

'They're paying us too well to refuse. I'll finally be able to think about upgrading the big pool. And there's a bonus in it for you. You start the day after tomorrow.'

'Why me?'

'Of course I'd send you. You're my best instructor. And you could do with a change in scenery.'

Gracie scoffed. 'I'm fine.'

Virginia raised an eyebrow.

Gracie drove her twenty-year-old car to and from the pool Wednesday through Sunday each week. She spent the days breathing in chlorine and her evenings with prune-like fingers, cooking, washing and helping her parents. Or sitting on her couch with Biscuit, her eight-year-old tabby. She was happy where she was.

But Gracie could hardly say no to Virginia, not only because she was her boss, but also because Virginia was her dearest and closest friend, the one person in the world in whom Gracie had ever confided her darkest and most shameful regrets.

'How long does he have to learn?'

'Two weeks.'

'Eeek.' That wasn't long. But if the man was healthy and coordinated, it might just be enough.

'And they need you to be available while they're filming in case he needs any additional help.'

'What does he have to learn?'

'To swim twenty metres or so, and tread water. There'll be some underwater shots, too. I'll email you the brief.'

It sounded doable.

'There are lots of contractual things to be aware of, NDAs and the like.'

Gracie suddenly saw where this was going as Virginia continued. 'But the thing that's really important to them is secrecy. No one can know that he's learning to swim. That he can't *already* swim. If you need to help him on set, you're to tell people you're his trainer, but no one is to know that he's a beginner. They've come to us for anonymity.'

'Not because we're good?'

'We're the best.' Virginia smiled. 'You're the best.'

Gracie dropped her head. She was good at her job. It was important. Each time she saw a report of a drowning, particularly of a child, her heart broke for the person and their family. Teaching some actor to swim, even for a movie role, was still teaching someone a skill for life.

But shame? Ego? She hated that. Plenty of people never had the chance to learn to swim. The stigma around it only made it harder for people to start, which in turn made them more likely to get into dangerous situations.

Gracie shook her head.

'It's no big deal,' Virginia said.

But it was to her. It was dishonest.

As an actor, this man was clearly all about his reputation and couldn't possibly be seen as less than perfect. She shook her head again.

'It's too much money to refuse. You know how tight things have been. We need this. And you're the best there is. I trust you more than anyone.'

And Gracie trusted Virginia. No one else had ever made her feel so safe and accepted.

'We won't get any publicity for the school, though,' Gracie pointed out archly. A lucrative contract was one thing, but publicity for White Horses for teaching a movie star would be infinitely greater.

Virginia shrugged. 'You can't have everything.'

No. You really couldn't. But Gracie didn't ask for much. Just some peace and quiet. A gentle life. One without drama. She'd had enough of that to last a lifetime.

'And what happens when he needs to swim longer distances?'

'Then you bring him here. After hours, I suppose. No one is to know he's getting swimming lessons, remember.'

'Virginia, seriously? There's no shame in not being able to swim. We need to remove the stigma so that more people come and get life-saving lessons.'

'I know. And ordinarily I'd agree, but this contract is worth too much money for us to refuse.'

White Horses was a successful swim school, but Virginia was hardly rolling in cash. After everything Virginia had done for Gracie over the years, how she'd been a supportive boss and best friend and confidant when everything else in her life was falling apart, Gracie would do anything for her. And Virginia knew it.

'I don't have a choice, do I?'

'You don't have a choice, because you have a

conscience. I know you. You believe in this place. And you believe in teaching everyone to swim, so of course you will say yes.'

'Okay.' She sighed. The two weeks would go by quickly.

'It'll be fun!' Virginia said.

'If your idea of fun is helping celebrities to lie?'

'Don't be silly. A change is as good as a holiday, and we all know you don't take enough of those.'

She didn't, but what was the point? What would she do all day? This was where she wanted to be. She loved her job, and as far as she was concerned, it was a gift, not a burden.

'What will you wear?' Virginia asked.

Gracie groaned. 'This!' She pointed to her uniform. Black shorts and one of her many yellow rash vests with the White Horses logo emblazoned across the front. 'My rashie!'

'You don't have to always wear that, you know.'

'Why would I wear anything else?' Gracie said, though suspected this was yet another gentle attempt by Virginia to encourage her to 'get out there,' wherever 'there' was. Gracie was perfectly happy either being at home in her garden with her cat or at the pool. It wasn't a big life, but it was big enough for Gracie.

'Just have fun,' Virginia insisted.

'Aye, aye, Boss.' Gracie tipped her head and turned. Her first lesson of that day was due to start.

'Gracie?'

'Yes?'

'You didn't even ask who he was.'

*He's just like any other client. Just like any other client.*

Gracie stood by her comment of two days earlier and was wearing her usual work outfit. She didn't want him thinking she was making any special effort for him. She'd dressed as she always did.

She pulled over to the side of the road and checked the address again. She was unfamiliar with the winding streets of the far eastern suburbs, with large fences partially obscuring even larger houses. She was in the right place. The house was not even visible behind the high brick wall, though the street number was subtly written by the gate.

She climbed out of her ancient hatchback and felt momentarily self-conscious about parking it on a street like this. Every car she'd passed in this suburb was less than a few years old. Hers was being held together by the dirt she hadn't been bothered to wash away.

*You don't care what he thinks! He's ashamed of having swimming lessons, remember?*

He was also, as Google had repeatedly told her, the best kisser in the world.

*That* was the one thing she was really trying hard not to think about.

Connor Day, world famous movie star, was gorgeous, blond-haired, blue-eyed, tall and broad-shouldered. He'd had his big break playing the loveable yet foolish foil to a cleverer brother in a series of movies about two brothers who find out they are actually aliens and have superpowers. Sort of slapstick supermen. Wildly successful and very silly. She'd only seen the first one.

He'd also been the lead in a few romantic comedies, including one featuring what the internet had proclaimed to be 'The Sexiest Kiss of All Time' with his co-star and girlfriend, Amanda Kim.

Gracie didn't know how the internet could judge if a kiss was the sexiest of all time, but even she had to admit that the kiss did leave Amanda Kim looking as though she couldn't remember her own name.

A bubble of nervousness filled Gracie's stomach, which was ridiculous. Gracie had taught hundreds of people how to swim, so a healthy adult should be no big deal at all.

Connor was simply a person who, for one reason or another, had never learnt. There were many reasons, cultural, financial. Personal. Fear. She didn't judge. The fact that someone had said 'I want to learn' was good enough for her.

Besides, he was a pretty blond, famous for playing a fool and for a pretty good kiss. He was not known for doing anything remotely serious. She had nothing to feel nervous about.

She hooked her bag over her shoulder and pressed the intercom. The gate rolled open at the pace of a giant turtle, not helping the anticipation rising annoyingly in her belly.

*Just like any other client.*

Finally the gate was open and *oh*.

There he was, right in front of her. Standing in the small courtyard beyond the high wall. Despite telling herself over and over that Connor Day was just like any other person, her limbs began to tingle. She wasn't expecting him to answer the door. She'd supposed he'd have an assistant for that. Or security. She hadn't expected him, alone, wearing shorts and a white T-shirt. Looking like he'd just rolled out of bed.

Or like he should roll straight back into it.

*Argh. No.*

They were right—movie stars did look different to ordinary mortals. Connor was practically glowing, as though he had his own internal light source. Vibrant, vital.

And then he smiled at her, and her heart might have stopped.

Damn. She didn't want to react like this. She was not a starstruck teenager. Or even a starstruck thirty-three-year-old. She was a practical, sensible woman who gave swimming lessons for a living.

A practical, sensible woman who had not been with a man in a while…

She had had a few casual relationships, but men tended to want more than she was willing to give. She hadn't had a serious relationship since she broke off her engagement to Matt six or seven years ago.

'Grace?'

She nodded while she swallowed and regained her voice. 'Yes. But call me Gracie. Everyone else does. Nice to meet you.'

'Good to meet you too, Gracie.' He stepped towards her, still smiling. Oh, that smile. It was so blinding she didn't see at first he was holding out his hand for her to shake.

Once she realised that was what he was doing, she lifted her hand, but missed his and hit his lower stomach. Because the other thing about Connor Day was that he was tall.

And Gracie was not. She didn't have much change left over from five feet, so most people in the world were taller than she was, but Connor was well over six foot.

His eyes ran up and down her body, assessing. No. Counting.

She recognised the expression in his eyes.

*You're short*, it said.

She stiffened, but he didn't seem to notice. Tall people never did.

'We can't both be nervous,' he said, holding her hand properly in both of his and steadying her. It felt as though he were wrapping her entire body in a hug.

Which was irritating because she was annoyed with him, first for the secrecy surrounding the lessons and then for the silent judgement about her height.

'Come on in,' he said, and started across the courtyard to the front door. She dutifully followed.

Connor Day might have been gorgeous, but that didn't mean he was a nice person. It didn't mean she wanted to be here.

*You don't have a choice. You owe it to Virginia.* As soon as the heavy door clicked closed behind her, Gracie began her prepared speech.

'As you know, I'm Gracie Sutherland. I work for the White Horses Swim School, and I've been a swimming instructor for fifteen years. You should also know I'm not just going to teach you how to pretend to swim. I'm going to teach you to *actually* swim. And basic CPR.'

He nodded. 'Thank you. I've been told you're the best.'

Her skin warmed. She'd expected more resistance but didn't find any.

'I'd like to start by getting to know your history,' she said.

He ran his hand through his gorgeous thick hair, giving her a ringside seat to his perfect bicep. 'Well, I was born in Boston. I started modelling when I was seventeen and acting when I was twenty, and—'

'Thanks, but I actually meant, what is your history with swimming? With the water. What can you do? What can't you do?'

'I can't do much. Nothing, really.' A blush coloured his golden cheeks, and irritatingly she began to soften. She reminded herself that it was never someone's fault if they hadn't learnt to swim. Connor, for all his privileges and gifts, should be no exception to this rule.

'Have you had any bad experiences in the water?' she asked gently.

'How bad?'

*Near drowning. Drowning. Struggling to pull your sister's lifeless body out of a hotel pool.*

'Anything that might have made you reluctant to get into the water?'

He shook his head.

'Good.' Part of her tension unravelled; teaching people who had had a traumatic experience like hers was her least favourite part of the job. It was vitally important, but that didn't make it easy.

'Are you comfortable in the water?' she asked.

'If I can touch the bottom.'

'Can you put your face in the water?'

He scoffed. 'Yes.'

'There's no need to be ashamed.'

'I'm not,' he said at the same time he crossed his arms.

'Okay,' she said in a tone that indicated she was anything but. 'Can you please show me the pool?'

He led her through a predictably beautiful house with hardwood floors, light-filled spaces, and large walls hung with elegant artwork and outside to a lush green garden.

She swallowed when she saw the pool. It was beautiful and stretched from one end of the yard to the other, a good long size. At one end was a pool house, white, open on three sides, with a large lounge and tables. But the part that stole her breath was the view beyond the pool. The property backed onto the harbour. Not the famous section with the bridge and Opera House, but the lesser-known but no less beautiful eastern harbour, with its secluded bays and stretches of unspoiled bush. His house overlooked Watsons Bay. Across the harbour was the suburb of Mosman and the headland that was home to Taronga Zoo.

'Will this be okay?' he asked. She took from his cheeky grin that he spoke with a heavy dose of sarcasm.

'I suppose we'll be able to make do,' she replied.

'Have I done anything to offend you?'

Gracie ground her teeth. Ignoring emotions and conflict was more her style, but it seemed that Connor was a get-it-all-out-there type of person, which was another strike against his name.

'Why do you say that?' she asked.

'You seem like you might be annoyed about something. But I don't know you very well, so I'm not sure, which is why I asked.'

She was usually so good at hiding her feelings. She'd had plenty of practice.

'There's nothing to be ashamed about, you know, not being able to swim. It doesn't need to be a secret,' she said.

Connor closed his eyes in a long blink. When he reopened them, his expression was steely.

'I'm not ashamed. But my manager thought it would be better for the film and my career for it not to get out. This is an important role for me.'

'A lot of people don't or can't learn to swim for many reasons, and there shouldn't be a stigma around it,' she continued. Battling nonsense like this was one of the biggest hurdles stopping people taking lessons.

The steel slowly melted from his face. He gave her a lopsided grin, which nearly undid her.

'I agree there shouldn't be a stigma. And as I said, I'm not ashamed I never had the opportunity to learn, but in this case, I have to do what my manager and the producers think is best for the film.'

She exhaled. Maybe she had misread him. At least it didn't seem to be his choice. But that wasn't the only thing bugging her.

'I'm also well aware that I'm not tall. I've had it pointed out to me almost daily all my life, just in case I didn't realise it myself.'

His golden face turned red.

'Gracie, I…didn't… Look, if you must know, when I saw you, I was instantly self-conscious about *my* height. I was wondering if… I mean, I'm a lot taller than you, and you're meant to be teaching me swimming. What would happen if I…' His voice faltered. For the briefest of seconds, she regretted making an issue of it.

'Get into trouble?'

'Yes.'

'Trust me, I could save you if you were drowning.' Gracie had made it a point to be strong enough to pull anyone out of the water, no matter their size, but she had to acknowledge that Connor didn't know this.

He nodded and had the decency to look sheepish.

'We should get started,' she said briskly. 'Do you want to get changed?'

'Of course. And there's a spare room if you want to get changed as well.'

Gracie looked down at herself. 'This is what I wear to teach. It protects me from the sun. It's necessary, especially when you're in the water for so long each day.'

'Oh, I…'

'You should consider wearing a rashie as well, particularly as we're outside. Are you wearing sunscreen?'

'How long will we be?'

'I don't know exactly, but let's assume it'll be long enough to get burnt.'

'Okay.'

'I'm serious about my job,' she said. 'I'm not sure what you expected.'

'This is exactly what I expected,' he said. 'I honestly want to learn to swim.' Connor turned and left like a dog with his tail between his legs.

Damn Virginia. She owed Gracie a raise. And a bonus. And a night out. She was so close to just grabbing her things and walking out of there and leaving someone else to teach Connor Day how to swim.

# CHAPTER TWO

CONNOR FELT OUT of his depth, and he hadn't even gotten into the water yet.

Gracie Sutherland was not exactly what he'd been expecting.

His first thought was that there was nothing to her. How could someone as slight as she was possibly teach a big oaf like him how to swim? He hadn't meant to offend her with his reaction to her height, but somehow he had. He'd also apparently managed to offend her in ways he wasn't aware of.

Connor's livelihood depended on his ability to hide his real emotions and project what the world wanted him to be, but Gracie had thrown him entirely off balance.

He was already nervous enough about this whole thing as it was. A judgemental swim instructor was the last thing he needed.

The second thing he'd noticed was that she was gorgeous—but he prided himself on having a strong immune response to attractive women. He had to. He worked with some of the most beautiful people in the world. He'd long since learnt to look past something as insignificant as someone's appearance and to their personality beyond. Attractive didn't always equal kind. Or intelligent. Or even good fun.

He'd been judged his whole life by his appearance. As long as he could remember, people had told him how good-looking he was. It was something he didn't even think about until he'd realised that people didn't say it to his mother or his brother or anyone else he knew.

No one else had modelling agents come up to them in the street and slip business cards into their hands.

That sort of thing only happened to Connor, and admittedly some of the people he'd modelled alongside and later acted with. But even in the world of show business, a discovery story like his was rare. Appearances mattered far less than anything else, including height, and Connor's unintentional reaction to Gracie's height made him cringe now as he pulled on his swimming shorts.

They'd gotten off on the wrong foot, and he wanted to make amends. But Gracie seemed immune to his charms. He wasn't a fool. He knew not everyone liked him. Many people thought he was a silly chump like the hapless character Jasper Dangerfield he'd played for too many years, but people didn't usually take an instant dislike to him as Gracie had. He wasn't sure how to deal with that.

Apart from anything else, he was looking forward to learning to swim. He would be able to wade out into the surf and keep walking until his feet lifted from the sand without assessing each wave so closely. He wouldn't get tripped up and show the world he was just a poor kid who was struggling to remember all the lies he'd told in his life.

He was looking forward to diving into swimming pools with confidence rather than sitting on the edge with his feet dangling in. Not checking which was the shallow end and easing himself into that.

It was exhausting, particularly in LA, where everyone he knew had a pool. Mostly they didn't swim in them. They were for status only. Heck, he had a massive pool himself. That he only ever looked at.

Gracie was waiting outside when he returned in his swimsuit. Her face was not made up, her dark hair was pulled back low and tight, and she was still wearing those old shorts and a hideous neon-yellow top. A streak of white zinc covered her nose, and a funny little bucket hat sat on her head.

Her outfit was unflattering to begin with, but once she'd smeared her face with white zinc and put the hat on, she looked almost eccentric.

Gracie didn't look or dress like any other trainer he'd ever had. And this was the person who was meant to be able to haul him out of the water if he sank?

*She's the best.*

That's what his manager, Bruce, had said when he'd told Connor about the arrangements. But Gracie clearly wasn't happy about the idea of secrecy, and he hadn't anticipated that.

*Maybe she wants the world to know that she's giving Connor Day swimming lessons?*

No.

That wasn't it. She didn't seem hungry for fame or notoriety. She seemed like one of those people—and he'd met many of them—who were at pains to express how much they *didn't* care about his fame. But there was something there, hidden by the shield of nonchalance she had created around herself. Almost like a protective force field.

*You didn't make a good first impression on her, either.*

Despite telling himself repeatedly that not being able to swim was nothing to be ashamed of, it had only taken one or two questions from her to get his back up.

But that didn't mean he wanted the whole world to know. Particularly his mother. She'd made so many sacrifices for him over the years. Paying for swimming lessons was one extra burden he'd refused to put on her. Not when there was rent due, when his brother needed a prescription filled. When the electricity was about to be cut off.

If it had only been about upsetting his mother, he might have been able to confess to Gracie, but it was far more than that. It was about his father discovering all the harm he'd done to his wife and children. It was about all the secrets Connor had been forced to keep for the safety of his mother and brother. It was about the bland profile on his Wikipedia page attesting to the normal upbringing he'd had, which was another lie he had to tell to keep his mother and brother safe.

He'd never told anyone he couldn't swim. Not ever. Not until he'd been approached by director Gerry Johns to play this role, and he'd realised that his character was going to have to swim a short distance. He'd taken a deep breath and phoned the person he trusted most in the world after his mother, his manager Bruce, and had explained the situation. Bruce had taken care of everything with his usual discreet efficiency.

Ten-year-old Connor could not have guessed that this lie would come back to bite him twenty-five years later on the other side of the world, as he stood by a sparkling pool next to this unusual woman, in her funny hat and warrior-like zinc cream.

'Do we get in now?' he asked.

She shook her head. 'Before we even get into the water, we need to go over the ten rules of water safety.'

She handed him a sheet of laminated paper. In

large print were indeed ten rules listed. He wanted to hand it back to her. He knew all about water safety. He'd been avoiding water all his life. No one knew how to avoid the water better than he did, but he sensed she was deeply serious about this, so he said nothing and kept hold of the sheet.

'Would you like to read them, or shall I?' she asked.

'Aloud?'

'Yes. That way I know you've understood.'

Did she think he couldn't even read? The look he gave her must have conveyed the question.

'I have to ask everyone. I assume you can read, but I like to hear my students say the rules out loud. It's nothing personal. Water safety is very important.'

He shouldn't have jumped to the conclusion that she was calling him stupid so quickly, but when you'd been called a himbo so many times…

'Okay. "Rule one. Walk, don't run,"' he read.

'The surface around a pool is slippery.'

'"Rule two. Obey instructions. Rule three. No roughhousing." Exactly how raucous do you think I'm going to get?'

She drew a deep breath. 'These rules are for everyone. At all times.'

Connor pressed his lips together and decided he didn't want to mess with her. But it was difficult.

'"No diving in the shallow end. Don't play with drains and covers. Use pool equipment properly.

Get out of the pool when storms threaten. Sun safety is part of the deal. Never drink alcohol and swim.'" He smiled at her and put down the sheet.

'And the last one?' she asked.

He picked it up again.

'It's one of the most important,' she prompted him.

'"Never swim alone,"' he read. 'Not ever?'

'Not ever.' She looked away and fussed in her bag but came up empty-handed. 'So you mustn't practice when you're alone here, understand?'

He nodded. He wasn't about to get in any pool with no one else around. After all the years of avoiding the water, he didn't need to be told that.

'Join me over here,' she said, and walked over to the pool. It was the shallow end, he knew, because it was always something he checked when he was around a new pool. So he'd know which end he had a fighting chance of surviving in.

Gracie sat on the edge with her feet in the water and looked at him.

This was a good thing. And not just because of the role. Because it was about time he got past this fear and learnt a skill that everyone else he knew seemed to have been born knowing.

It would be a relief.

And yet before he could celebrate, he had to get into the damn pool.

Gracie looked up at him with her awful yellow

shirt and funny hat. She did not look strong enough to pull him out of the water, and yet…

He walked over to the side of the pool and sat on the concrete next to her.

'Do you feel comfortable putting your feet in?' she asked.

Of course! It wasn't like he'd never been in a pool, though he was careful to stay where he could stand. He looked into her eyes. For the first time, they were at the same level as his, and they looked different. Not defiant and challenging as they did when she looked up at him, but curious and sympathetic.

Connor swung his feet over the edge, holding on to the side with hands he was ashamed to find were shaking. He dipped his feet into the water and gasped.

Gracie laughed softly. 'You'll get used to it, and at least this pool seems to be heated. The worst part will be your groin. That's the true indication of temperature.'

Connor jolted. He wasn't unfamiliar with the sensation of being waist-deep in cold water, but had she just made a joke? Not a funny one, but it seemed she did have a less serious side.

Something inside him began to crack, and he knew that he could trust Gracie and her funny hat.

'I do feel comfortable standing in water if it isn't too deep,' he offered.

'Great,' she said, and slipped into the water in

one fluid movement. Momentarily focused on her legs and bottom and the ease with which she lifted them to slip into the water, he wasn't checking the depth of the water when he followed her in. He landed awkwardly. Gracie grabbed his arm, stopping him from falling face first into the water.

'Sorry,' he muttered, heart racing.

'Nothing to be sorry about. Are you okay?'

He nodded, even though his heart was still in his throat.

'We'll start with floating and treading water,' she said.

'I don't need to know that.' He needed to learn how to swim, not muck around.

'Everyone should know how to do that. Though…'

Her eyes travelled over his torso, and his skin prickled. He was aware of her judgement.

*Just a himbo…*

'Not everyone can float easily. But we'll give it a go.'

Floating meant lifting his feet and turning his face from the water. Wouldn't he just sink?

'People who aren't relaxed or who are particularly…solid find it more difficult.' She coughed. 'We can assume that's you.'

'I'm relaxed.'

She raised an eyebrow.

Who was he kidding? He might not have been a quivering mess, but he was hardly relaxed. His fingers were still tingling from the near miss a few minutes ago.

'But you're…dense. I mean, your body is very muscular.'

Ah. So Gracie Sutherland wasn't as nonchalant and unaffected as she was pretending to be. That was interesting and somehow made him relax a little more.

'Do you think you could put your face in the water?'

'Of course.'

She stood and looked at him. After a while she said, 'Come on, then.'

'Now?'

'If you're comfortable.'

He wasn't, but waiting wasn't going to make him more so.

He bent down.

The problem with the height differential was that whereas Gracie only needed to duck her body slightly to submerge her face, Connor had to bend right over. He was surprised by how far he had to lean. By the time he felt his body toppling over, it was too late. He slipped, struggled, thrashed his arms, coughed on a mouthful of water, but a second later was tugged upright and found himself staring into a pair of wide brown eyes. If the water hadn't knocked his breath from him, then the sunlight catching on the shards of gold in Gracie's pretty eyes as she looked at him certainly did.

'Are you okay?' she asked.

His limbs tingled, and his throat was scratchy from coughing, but once he caught his breath, he said, 'Only embarrassed. I didn't realise I had to lean so far forward.'

'Don't be. I'm sorry. You aren't used to the weight of the water, and it threw you off balance. Wait a sec.'

She lifted herself out of the water in a smooth motion and went to her bag. She slipped back into the pool carrying a red ball about the size of a tennis ball.

'Catch this,' she said, and threw it to him gently. He caught it.

She held up her hands, and he threw it back to her. 'Is this your first time in Sydney?' she asked.

'No, I've been before on promo trips, but this is my first time really working here. I love it.' He tossed back the ball.

'How long are you staying?'

'It depends, but filming is scheduled to take around six weeks, and we start in around two, so... maybe two months?'

She moved into the deeper water and threw him the ball as she did so. He threw it back.

'Tell me about LA. Were you born there?'

'Ah, no.' He caught the ball again and realised she was just doing this to get him comfortable. He both resented and appreciated the sentiment. How was it possible to have so many conflicting feelings about one person? 'I already told you I was born in Boston. I moved to New York when I was eighteen and LA two years after that.'

'Wow, what's Boston like?'

'Have you been to the States?' he asked, throwing the ball back.

She shook her head once. 'Nope.'

He wasn't sure why, but he got the impression she wouldn't care to. Which was odd considering she seemed genuinely interested in his responses to her questions.

'And Boston?' she prompted.

'Boston is…' He hesitated. There were too many memories to give her just a sound bite. Mostly good, but many complicated.

'Boston's great. I don't get back there as much as I'd like.'

She nodded, caught the ball and tossed it to him again.

'Do you still have family there?'

'My mum, my brother and his family.'

'Your dad?'

He shook his head in the same curt way she had. 'Long gone.'

She got the message.

Long gone and hopefully not making some other woman's life hell like he had his mother's.

Sinead Day had left a marriage that had deteriorated from apparently loving to controlling and angry. Sinead had taken both boys and fled.

His father had fought hard for custody, not because he loved his children but, Connor suspected, as a further way to manipulate and control his mother. If his father had cared at all for his children, he wouldn't have driven them further and further into poverty. First to a studio apartment and then finally to his mother's car. It had only been for four months and luckily not over a cold New England winter, but fathers who loved their children didn't fight their ex-wives so hard in court that they were left destitute.

Not that Connor's father ever knew they were living in the car. No one did. Because if anyone had known, then his father would have been able to argue that Sinead was not a good mother and that the children must live with him. If there was one lesson Connor had learnt over that time, it was how to keep a secret.

How to bend the truth.

Because no one could ever know they were living in the car, or Connor and his brother would be taken from their mother. No one could know they didn't have enough to eat, or they would be taken from their mother. No one could know she couldn't afford swimming lessons. No one could know any of it.

He realised he'd been standing there holding the ball for a while too long.

'Are you sure you're okay?' she asked.

'Yes, sorry.' He blinked in the bright Sydney

sun. 'I'm feeling much more comfortable, ready to show you I can put my face in the water without stumbling.'

She smiled. 'Let's try blowing some bubbles.'

'Like a baby?'

'No, like someone learning to swim.'

'I know,' he said, wishing he believed himself.

'It isn't your fault you never learnt as a kid,' she said.

Except it was. It had been his choice. His lie. White, because he told it to be kind. White because he didn't want to upset his mother.

Gracie took him to the side of the pool. 'Hold on to the edge and steady yourself. Then put your face in the water.'

Gracie stood near him. Within reach, but she didn't touch him, and he was acutely aware of that. And the fact that he wanted her to.

He did as he was told and this time managed to submerge his face and blow air out of his mouth, making bubbles, without slipping.

'Lift your head up, take a deep breath, and repeat the bubbles.'

He did as he was told several times and then took his hand off the wall and did it again. He lifted his face and let the water fall from his eyes. When he could focus again, he looked at Gracie, and his stomach swooped when he saw her wide smile.

'Well done. How do you feel about floating on your back?'

*Terrified*, he thought, but he nodded.

'Back floats are one of the most important skills after breathing. It's a safety position. Once you know how to float, you will feel much more comfortable in the water. An important thing to remember is to tilt your chin back. If your chin is out of the water, your nose and mouth will be too. Okay?'

'Okay,' he said.

'The other thing to remember is to spread your arms and legs out wide. And look, there's no other way to say this, but squeeze your cheeks and push your pelvis up.'

'I assume you don't mean the cheeks on my face?'

'No, I do not.'

He caught the shadow of a grin crossing her face but made nothing of it. They'd talked about his groin and his butt, but she was a professional, and he wanted to show her that he was too.

'Would you like me to show you?' she asked.

'How you squeeze your cheeks?'

Her face turned pink under the zinc cream. 'I meant the back float.'

'Oh, yes, of course. Sorry.'

'But if…you need…'

'Please, show me the back float.'

Gracie didn't even bother taking her hat off,

lifted her feet and lay back down in the water as though she were lying on a bed.

But she was petite, and he could see, even through her shirt, that her stomach muscles were strong, her core tight. She had her eyes closed, and she looked…peaceful. He was so busy watching her face, he missed almost everything else. She opened her eyes and stood back up.

'We can take it slowly, and I'll stand right here. You aren't going to drown.'

'So it's like a trust fall?'

'Exactly.'

'And will you catch me?'

'Of course I will, if needed. But the water can hold you. Yes, even you.'

Her gaze darted up and down his body again, from his waist to his shoulders, though not, he noticed, as far as his eyes. Keeping fit and strong was part of his job description. If he hadn't needed to maintain his body for work, he doubted he'd have been so disciplined. But yes, he was told regularly that he was well-built. A fact that Gracie's eyes were reminding him of.

'Chin up, arms and legs out, squeeze and relax. Do you want to try it?'

The thought petrified him, but he had to do it. If only to prove to Gracie that he was not going to be able to float and they could skip this step.

*She'll catch you.*

She would, or die trying to get her five-foot frame to drag his six-four one out of the pool.

He closed his eyes, lifted his feet and…

Sank. Connor's bottom fell, pulling the rest of him after it.

Once his face went under, he scrambled for footing and was aware of a firm hand under his shoulders, lifting him.

'I told you…'

He steadied his body and his heart with deep breaths, but Gracie's hand remained on his arm. Her reassurance should have calmed him, but his pulse still fluttered.

'Nonsense. You just didn't do as I said. You didn't squeeze your butt. Or spread your arms.'

He bit back a smile. She was bossy. He liked it. He liked that she wasn't afraid to tell him what he was doing wrong.

'Chin up, arms out, pelvis up. But this time look me in the eye.'

This time Gracie took his shoulders and eased him back into the water. 'Keep looking at me. I've got you. And relax.'

Relaxing was nigh on impossible with Gracie's hands small but firm under his shoulders and waist. It was proving to be quite difficult.

*You're an actor, so act.*

Except he wasn't a very good actor. He was a pretty face with an okay body and a massive dose of luck.

His bottom began to sink, pulling the rest of him down with it.

'Squeeze!' she urged, and he tried. 'Pelvis up!'

It worked. He wasn't flat by any means, but his face was kept out of the water. He held the position for a few moments and then managed to place his feet back on the bottom without going under first.

It was hard work. He lost track of time as she got him to try floating again, then bubbles, then floating. She got him to hold on to the side of the pool and practice kicking, and then he progressed to a kickboard.

He stretched and yawned. It wasn't an exaggeration to say he was feeling muscles he hadn't realised he had.

Gracie checked her watch. 'It's been over two hours. I think that's probably enough for today.'

'That went well.' Then, in a moment of doubt, he added, 'Did it go well?' He had no idea. He was certainly getting more comfortable in the water but also more worked up each time he felt Gracie touch his arm. Or his shoulder. Or simply the sensation of the water pushing against him whenever she moved near him.

She laughed. 'The lesson went well, yes. I'm sure we'll have you swimming laps in no time.'

Laps of a pool? That seemed almost impossible. Yet many of the things that had happened in his life had seemed impossible at first. And then they had happened. And then they had become commonplace. Flying in a private jet, working with award-winning actors. Being invited to exclusive parties. Living in the Hollywood Hills.

Pretending to be someone else came naturally to a kid who wanted to be anyone but who he really was. A poor kid with no father, an overworked mother, a younger brother who took up what little energy his mother had to spare.

Pretending to be able to do things he couldn't, being someone else, became more than a way to get noticed and then make money. Pretending to be someone else became a way of life.

They got out of the pool. He showed her to the guest bathroom, where she could shower and change. When she came out, she was wearing jeans and a black T-shirt, the horrible yellow top nowhere to be seen. Her long hair was damp but loose.

Out of the ugly shirt, with the zinc cream and bucket hat removed, she was…gorgeous. His breath caught.

She nodded when she saw him, but her face was impassive. He felt his pulse in his throat. Gracie Sutherland kept surprising him.

'Are you going to be able to teach me?' he asked.

'I already am, aren't I?' She pulled a face.

'You seemed a little defensive to begin with.'

'Only because….' Her words faltered. 'Are you always this forward?'

He gave her his best grin. One that had landed

him several roles and more than a few first dates. 'I prefer to think of myself as curious. I imagine you don't coach many other movie stars.'

'I have plenty of clients from all different backgrounds,' she said.

'But ever an actor? Or someone famous?'

'I once taught the brother of our local MP.'

'I'm going to take that as a no.'

'Fine, I've never taught anyone famous.'

'I'm just like you, you know,' he said.

'Ha! This house is not like any I've ever seen before. That pool, the view.' She waved her arms in the direction of the harbour.

'They aren't mine.'

She shook her head. 'They certainly aren't mine. Same time tomorrow?'

He showed her out and said, 'Tomorrow you should drive in the gate. Buzz and I'll let you in.'

He watched her drive her old hatchback down the street. He couldn't figure her out. She was obviously annoyed at the secrecy of the lessons, but she was also very businesslike. Professional. Except for those few moments he'd caught her looking at his body. Had she been admiring him or just studying him as one of her students? And why did it even matter?

*You're just put out because she's not fawning over you like practically every other woman you meet.*

Not every woman.

Connor checked the clock. It would be late in Boston, but knowing his mother, who hardly slept, she'd still be awake. He put through a video call.

'Connor, darling! I'm so glad you called. I'm at Callum and Yumi's.'

His sister-in-law moved into view of the screen. 'Connor! I'm trying to get Hana into bed. Do you mind?'

He smiled and shook his head. Then his niece, Hana, pushed her grandmother out of the way and said, 'Connor! How's Sydney?'

He spent the next ten minutes telling his mother, sister-in-law and niece about Sydney, giving them a virtual tour of the house and the view.

'What a gorgeous spot. Have you been swimming?' Hana asked.

'I have, actually,' Connor said, and he loved how that wasn't even a lie.

He ended the call feeling lighter than he had for ages.

It had felt good to say it. *I went for a swim.*

# CHAPTER THREE

THE NEXT DAY'S lesson went smoother than the first.

For starters, Connor was now wearing a black rashie. She knew she should be pleased he was covering up his skin in the late summer sun, but a little part of her was sad she wasn't getting another close-up of his spectacular torso, sculptured arms and smooth skin the colour of golden honey.

*You'll have to watch one of his movies tonight.*

She chided herself. Yesterday she was convinced he was a jerk, but today she wanted to ogle him. Hopefully by tomorrow her feelings would average out to mild nonchalance and she'd be able to finish his lessons without becoming too worked up about anything much at all.

They went over everything from the day before, and thankfully Connor hadn't forgotten anything. She had him practice floating on his back again, from standing, from pushing back from the wall and then rolling over.

'This is the foundation for front crawl or freestyle. Do you think you can hold on to the wall with one hand while pointing the other hand out at me?'

Connor did exactly that and remembered to blow bubbles as he did so. *Star pupil*, she thought. *Literally.* She smiled to herself. Luckily his face was still in the water, and he didn't see her dopey expression.

Next they sat on the side of the pool, and she demonstrated the arm movements of first freestyle and then breaststroke.

'Copy me,' she said.

Connor lifted his arm up but didn't bend his elbow gently as she'd shown him.

'Some people call it a catch and pull, but you aren't catching anything. The flatter your hand is, the greater surface area you'll have, which gives you more power.'

He tried again, but the angles were wrong.

'May I?' she asked as she reached for his arm. He nodded.

She attempted to show him by gently moving his arm into the correct position. Connor's skin was slippery, his body warm. His muscles so much harder than those of any other pupil she'd ever taught. Her fingertips leapt back in surprise.

Thankfully his next movements were closer to being correct. She said, 'You catch on quickly. That's good.'

'I've had to take many dancing lessons and learn

stunts. This isn't exactly like that, but it isn't *not* like that either.'

He smiled at her, and her throat closed.

She coughed and said a little hoarsely, 'Good thing too. We'll have you swimming like a pro in no time, and then you'll be rid of me.'

She wasn't sure why she'd added the last line. *She'd* be finished with *him*, was what she really meant. Teaching someone as attractive as Connor was not a problem she'd ever foreseen herself having.

She'd always had a thing for blond men, ever since Danny James in fourth grade. He was cute and funny, and when she'd returned to school after Caroline had died, he'd given her a handmade card on which he'd written, 'I'm very sorry your sister is gone.' She'd had to go to the bathroom in tears, but she'd been so touched that Danny, who she really didn't know very well, had done that, when no one else had said anything to her.

*She watched her sister die*, is what she'd imagined them all saying.

But she couldn't put her attraction to one of the sexiest men alive completely down to Danny James.

Connor Day was objectively handsome, but he also had *that thing*. That extra thing super successful people have, regardless of how attractive they are. That thing that makes you want to be near them. He had more than the legal limit of it.

The March day was warmer than the one before, and an hour or so into the lesson, Gracie was already parched. She reached for her drink bottle, which she kept by the side of the pool, but Connor said, 'I've got cold water inside, if you'd prefer? Or I can make you a coffee, though I can't promise it'll be up to your Australian standards.'

'I'll take my chances,' she said, wanting a caffeine fix and a break from the sun.

Towelling herself off, she followed him into his kitchen, guiltily admiring the swing of his narrow hips as they went.

It was a funny thing, meeting someone who looked familiar but who you didn't actually know at all. She had to keep reminding herself that this man wasn't Jasper Dangerfield but Connor, a client and a stranger. All the characters he'd played were just in her head, messing with her thoughts.

She sat on a stool and watched as he poured a glass of ice-cold water from the fridge and then set to work with the coffee machine.

*Connor Day is making you coffee*, a voice whispered in the back of her head. *And he isn't even wearing pants!* She told that voice to shut up.

Never in her decade and a half of teaching swimming had her body reacted to a pupil the way it was now. She didn't want this. She didn't need this in her life. Her mind and body worked best when they were calm. Even.

The kitchen was huge, just like the rest of house.

Modern yet warm. Thoughtfully designed, bright and airy.

'Is it just you staying here?'

He arched a brow. 'That sounds like a relationship question.'

'What? No! That's none of my business.' She gulped the cold water. 'I only asked because the place is huge. I thought you might have an assistant or, I don't know, a friend, maybe.'

'Oh, right. Of course.' He frowned for an instant, but then his face returned to its usual gorgeousness. 'It's just me. Usually I'd stay in the hotel the rest of the cast and crew are in, but…'

'You needed the pool.'

'Yeah.' He had the decency to look sheepish. But not the decency to answer the question she'd posed: Was he in a relationship?

'Well, it's a nice place.'

He looked around the kitchen as though looking at it for the first time. 'Yes.'

'Silly me, your own place is probably way fancier and bigger than this.'

He shook his head. 'No, my house is smaller than this. Especially the pool.'

'You have a pool?'

He grimaced. 'Yeah, well, it's a nice house in the Hollywood Hills. They don't tend to make those without pools.'

He had a house with a pool that he couldn't use? She didn't know if that was funny or incredibly sad. Either way, she felt one sentence away from saying the wrong thing.

He put two mugs on the bench and sat across from her.

'Tell me about you?' he asked, as though she might have anything interesting to tell.

'There's not much to say. I teach swimming.'

'Great. For how long?'

'Um, over fifteen years. I started when I was a teenager.'

'And what made you want to do that?'

'It's an important life skill that people should learn.'

He nodded, and she hoped he was out of questions. But no.

'Have you always lived in Sydney?' he asked.

She must have pulled a face. Before she answered, he said, 'I don't mean to give you an interrogation. I'm just interested in people. Professional hazard.'

'Professional…what?'

'I try to understand people, and like to know what makes them tick. I'm sorry if I came across too intrusive.'

She bristled but said, 'It's okay. I'm just surprised.'

'You thought I'd be a brainless, ego-fuelled, stuck-up movie star?'

'No!'

He raised an eyebrow and was right to do so.

'This might come as a surprise to you, but I don't meet a lot of movie stars.' She grinned—she couldn't help it—and was met with a broad, twinkling smile in return. His eyes were the colour of the sky just before the last of the light faded, violet, dark blue, and with stars starting to appear.

And it would achieve nothing to focus on them or the way a wave of warmth was currently washing through her body.

'Are you filming near here?' she asked, proud of herself for changing the subject.

'Some. And at a studio close to the city, I think.'

'Will you get to do some sightseeing while you're in Australia?'

He shook his head. 'Probably not. Things will get pretty busy the week after next. Sixteen-hour days often.'

'Sounds exhausting.'

Gracie was almost out of conversation topics. She had no idea what to speak to a famous actor about. All she knew was that she didn't want to talk about herself.

'What's the film about?' she asked.

'It's a family drama about two couples struggling with grief over the loss of a child.'

The blood rushed from Gracie's head, and she reached for the bench.

'I know you probably think it sounds a bit boring. Not like what I usually do,' he said.

'That's not it. It doesn't sound boring. It sounds

harrowing.' And heartbreaking and distressing and not the sort of movie Gracie would want to see, but not for the reasons he thought.

'It's more emotional than projects I've done in the past, but I want to do something to stretch myself, something more challenging.'

Gracie's mind left her body for a moment, which was the only reason she could think of that would have made her mouth ask, 'Why do you need to learn to swim?'

'Because the child falls from some rocks and drowns in the ocean, and my character is the one who fails to save her.'

The room began to spin, and she wanted to throw up. Did Virginia know this when she sent her on this assignment? Surely not. If Virginia had known, Gracie would have been the last person she'd have chosen to teach Connor.

On wobbly knees, Gracie stood. *Fall. Ocean. Rescue. Fails.*

'You might need another teacher. I don't think I can do this.'

He blinked. 'Why not?' he said.

She looked around for her bag and her things, but was momentarily confused about where she was and where she'd left them. 'I just don't think I'm the right person to teach you how to do that.' She walked out of the kitchen into a room she hadn't been in before. She groaned. She had to get out of there!

'Is it me?' he asked. Connor stood in front of her and placed a hand gently on her shoulder. Not enough to stop her moving, just enough to send a little of his warmth into her chilled body and bring her out of her current state of confusion and fear.

'No, it isn't you.'

'You look pale. I think you should sit down.'

She was vaguely aware of strong arms leading her to a couch, where she was seated. Not long after, her glass of water was placed in her hand. It must have been Connor, but at that point, all she was aware of was her pounding heart and spinning head.

Moments later, he placed something else before her. A chocolate chip cookie on a plate. 'What?' she spluttered.

'Do you need something to eat? Gracie, what can I do?'

She stared at the cookie, and around the room, but nothing seemed to compute.

All she could think about was Caroline. The pool. Her body. Floating upside down. Screams. Flashing lights.

This wasn't the first time she'd had a panic attack like this. It wasn't even the first time this year, but it was unexpected. Being somewhere unfamiliar, it was more difficult to rein in than usual. She made herself go through the steps.

*Focus on something you can hear.* A bird outside. *Focus on something you can smell.* The chocolate in the cookie sitting in front of her. *Focus on something you can feel.* The soft leather of the couch under her bare thighs. *Focus on something you can see.* Connor's handsome face. He didn't say anything but sat close by calmly. Silently. Non-judgemental.

'I'm sorry,' she said.

'No, I'm sorry. I thought you needed sugar, but it was a panic attack, wasn't it?'

'Yes.' She nodded and tried to stand. She looked around the room, forgetting where she'd left her bag. Outside. By the pool. Wherever that was.

With a gentle hand, he nudged her back down onto the couch.

'Wait a moment. Whether you decide to teach me or not, you aren't going anywhere just yet. What do you usually do when this happens?'

'I rest for a while. Meditate. Breathe.'

'The coffee can wait. I'll get you an herbal tea and then leave you for a moment, okay? But you're not driving anywhere until you feel better.'

Concern creased Connor's face, and she knew he was right. She needed to rest. She closed her eyes and did her breathing exercises. When she opened her eyes, on the table in front of her was a pot of tea, a plate with more cookies and another plate with sliced up strawberries and crisp apple. Her heart skipped a few beats, which was unfortunate, as she'd just got her heart rate back under control. The only other person who had treated her attacks with such kindness and patience was Virginia. She almost hated to quit this job, yet she had to.

Gracie sipped some tea and ate the cookies and fruit. Once her limbs had stopped tingling and her feet were steady, she stood. Connor was in the next room but came to her when he saw her standing.

'Thank you for this, Connor. It was just what I needed, but I'm sorry. I still think it's best you get another teacher.'

'Can you at least tell me why?'

'It's not important.' She shook her head.

'You nearly passed out in my kitchen, and you hadn't even drunk my coffee yet. It isn't nothing.'

'Nothing you need to know about, then.'

'Okay, sure, but think of my poor fragile actor's ego. If you don't tell me, I'll take it personally.' He smiled the kind of smile that made his teeth dazzle and the edges of his eyes crinkle, and she couldn't help but smile back.

Connor nodded to the couch, and she let herself sink back into it. It was a very comfortable couch.

'When I was ten years old, I watched my younger sister drown. She was eight.'

He nodded but left the air empty for her to fill.

'It was my fault. We were on holiday. My parents said I couldn't go swimming in the hotel pool, but I snuck out anyway. Caroline followed me. I didn't realise until it was too late.'

'You were only ten.'

'But I wasn't meant to go. I disobeyed my parents. No one else there was able to pull her out.'

As much as she'd tried to tell herself if wasn't her fault, her parents never had. It was clear to her that they blamed her.

'You were just a kid.'

It was a refrain she'd heard from many well-meaning people over the years. But it was pointless.

'I wasn't a baby.' She was old enough that she could remember everything about that day. Every thought. Every feeling. Every action.

'Ten still isn't a grown-up. I did some awful things when I was a kid,' he said.

Her throat burnt. No one really ever knew what it was like, but this was a new angle. And it was insensitive.

'Oh, yeah? Did anyone die?'

He looked down. 'I'm sorry. I didn't mean to trivialise what happened to you. I really didn't.'

'You don't get it. You seem like a caring person, Connor, but no one really gets it.'

'No, I don't. But I also don't blame little Connor for the things he did or thought he had to do.'

'Yeah, what did you do?'

Connor paused for a long while, but eventually shook his head. 'It's not important. What's important is that I really want to learn to swim. More than ever, after what you've just told me. Not because of the role. But because it's something I should do, particularly as I now have the chance and a wonderful teacher. I'd still like you to stay.'

Gracie's thoughts were a tumbled mess. She sometimes got like this after a panic attack. Exhausted, disoriented.

It would be easier if she just gathered her things and went home.

*You always take the easy way out.* That voice was Virginia's.

'Where are your parents now?' he asked.

'Sydney. Not far from where I live. We all moved here, after.'

'A change of scenery?'

'Something like that. Too many memories in the old house. Though you never really outrun them.'

'Are you close to your parents?'

That was a tricky question. 'I see them several times a week, talk to them most days.'

'That didn't sound like a yes.'

'Yes, I mean. Obviously we're close.'

She did so many things for them. Was their constant helper, and even though neither of them was particularly old, they depended on her. They needed her, which was why she'd never travelled far from home.

It was easier to keep to herself and build her own fortress. Her own space where she lived with Biscuit and where she could control what happened.

She imagined herself getting back into her car and driving back to White Horses and telling Virginia, the person who had supported her most in the world, that she couldn't do this job. Seeing the look on Virginia's face. The expression of disappointment might be worse than simply getting through the next week or two and sending Connor on his way. He was a good pupil. A very quick learner. And there were other perks to this job…

The cookies, for starters.

'I'd really like you to keep teaching me.' He stepped toward her. For the briefest of instants, she thought he might reach out to touch her. She leant back.

It wasn't as though they hadn't touched. She'd had the pleasure of touching his body many times over the past two days, accidentally and as part of her job, but this was different. They were far more vulnerable. They might have been out of the pool, but they had both laid their secrets out for the other to see and judge.

*He didn't judge you. He doesn't blame you.*

*He's one more person who needs to swim. Especially because he actually owns a pool.* She shuddered.

'Okay. But this pool won't do. We'll have to get you into the ocean.'

'The sea? I'm not ready,' Connor stammered. He'd only been in the pool for one and a half lessons, and now she wanted him to get into the ocean? One moment she was about to walk out his door and stop teaching him. The next she was telling him they were going to swim with the sharks.

Gracie drew a deep breath that seemed to infuse her with a new resolve. He'd been shaken as he'd watched her fall apart. She'd told him about her sister, the tragedy her family had gone through. He wasn't convinced by her story that her relationship with her parents was rosy. The way her face fell when she spoke about them told him more than her words.

Yet now, somehow, she'd gathered herself together and was heading back out to the pool. He had no choice but to follow her.

'Relax. Not the surf. The harbour will do. There are some gorgeous places around here. Secluded. Calm. Just the place to learn.'

'Yes, but…what if I'm seen?' *What if I can't do it? The ocean is vast and endless, and there are things swimming beneath the surface.*

'You'll say you're having a swim, just like anyone else.'

'Now?'

She laughed. It was a happy sound, particularly after the conversation they'd just had, when he'd been certain she was close to tears. It had taken him too long to realise what was wrong. He'd been too terrified to think properly. He should've made the link between their conversation about the film and her reaction sooner than he had.

He understood her a little better now. The no-

nonsense approach she had to her work and the reason she'd been so hesitant to speak about herself.

'No. After a few more lessons. But we shouldn't wait too long. You'll need to learn to be as comfortable swimming in salt water as a pool.'

'Thank you,' he said. As nervous as he was about being in a pool, it now worried him far less that the ocean he was going to have to be in to play the part.

Back in the water, Connor's mind was split in a million different directions. Yet all of them ended back at Gracie. It didn't help that she was next to him in the pool, her hands occasionally on his body, gently guiding his movements.

He was so aware of her presence next to him. At first, he needed her next to him for security, but as he became more comfortable in the water, it was something else. Desire.

It was hard enough learning to swim, let alone keeping his cool around Gracie, who was five feet of contradictions. Small yet unaccountably strong, determined yet hurting. He wanted to give both her parents a piece of his mind. The idea of letting a ten-year-old believe she was in any way responsible for her sister's death?

To assuage their own guilt, he guessed. It was a reason but not an excuse.

He tried his best to concentrate on what Gracie was telling him. She got him to hold on to the side of the pool, hold his legs out and kick. Once she was satisfied he'd mastered that, she took a kickboard out of her bag and had him practice again with that. He managed several lengths of the shallow end of the pool holding the kickboard and dutifully blowing bubbles.

Of course he was hyperaware of her. He was used to being watched, so used to it he was practically immune. He was even used to being judged as he was watched. But he was never this acutely aware of the person doing the watching. Gracie Sutherland was the last person he should have been attracted to. She wasn't an actress who understood the slightly different rules of show business relationships. She was not a celebrity accustomed to his strange world. Besides, they worked together. She was his teacher. A relationship he wasn't about to take advantage of.

Always travelling, working eighty-hour weeks or not at all. A swarm of photographers following him everywhere he went.

Hardly ideal conditions for a relationship, even if he were relationship material.

Which he was not.

So he'd have to admire Gracie from a distance and keep his cool when she was close.

Over the next few days, they settled into an easy routine. She would arrive in the morning. They would spend about an hour in the pool, then break for a coffee. 'Tolerable' was how she described his attempt at a flat white. Australians were so funny about their coffee, as protective as the French were with their wine or the Italians with their pizza.

He sensed she wasn't comfortable with him asking too many personal questions, so he asked her mainly about her work. She taught regular classes with kids and toddlers but also gave private lessons, including to people who had disabilities or health problems. In amongst all this, he did manage to learn that she lived alone with her cat. If there was a partner on the scene, they didn't live together.

Not that he cared. It was professional curiosity. That was all.

But at the end of that first week, as she was packing up her things to leave, she announced, 'Okay. You're ready for the salt water.'

# CHAPTER FOUR

THE AIR WAS fresh and heavy with morning dew. The sun was slowly making itself known in the dark blue sky. Gracie had picked Connor up around six in the morning when it was still dark and driven him a mile or so to this little beach on the harbour. Parsley Bay. As Gracie had promised, the water was flat and calm. Only a few other swimmers were here, engaged in their own morning exercise and oblivious to his presence.

The beach was narrow and faced an elongated bay stretching out to the rest of the harbour. Parsley Bay was sheltered and was spanned by a white suspension footbridge, linking the two cliffs at each side of the bay. It was beautiful, and improbable. Only a short distance from where he was staying and moments from the centre of Sydney, yet it felt like the middle of nowhere.

And the water didn't look terrifying. It almost looked inviting.

Connor had only been in the sea once before, and that was so long ago it barely counted. When his parents were still together. His father had tried to drag him into the sea one summer day on Cape Cod. Connor had screamed and resisted, but his father had tugged him in. Connor had been crying when his mother had pulled him back out. 'Sissy,' his father had taunted. 'Crybaby.'

Wow. He hadn't thought about that day in years. And it was the last thing he needed to be thinking about now. He shook his head, and the memory, away.

'Are there sharks here?' he asked.

'Yes, but no.'

'What does that mean?'

'There are sharks in the harbour itself, yes, but Parsley Bay has a shark net.'

'Does that mean they can't get in?'

'Probably. But also, it's the wrong time of day for them, and you'd have to be really unlucky.'

'I could be unlucky.'

She laughed. And was right to. While he hadn't led a life without struggle, the last two decades of his life had been fairy-blessed.

He trusted her. He could do this. Besides, he needed to make this movie. To show everyone he wasn't just a pretty face.

'There are no waves,' he noted.

'I told you,' she said, and smiled at him. Ever since her panic attack the other day, she'd relaxed more in his presence. She'd started to treat him like a regular person, which was a relief. But the dropping of her guard had also manifested a new level of feistiness that had him on his toes.

'This will be a gentle introduction to the ocean. You'll be filming some scenes there, won't you?'

He nodded.

They hadn't spoken about her sister since that morning. He was leaving it to her to bring up, but he was glad she'd decided to keep teaching him. Not just for his sake, but also for hers. She was carrying a lot of guilt. Even though he didn't have the first idea how to help unburden her of it, he wanted that for her.

'Let's go,' she prompted. When he didn't move, she added, 'It's calm, flat and clear. It's ideal. It'll feel different to the pool, and obviously you won't be just a few strokes from the edge, but I'm here.'

When she smiled at him, his stomach dipped. Her brown eyes were dark and soulful. Sometimes he had to remind himself to stop staring at them, because when he did, he forgot what she was telling him and what he was meant to be doing.

The sky was getting lighter. 'It's a gorgeous time of day, isn't it?' she said.

'Spectacular,' he agreed, looking out across the water to the first rays of sun hitting the ocean.

'I can't believe there's hardly anyone else here,' he added. 'If I could swim, I'd be here every day.'

'You will be able to swim. Very soon. There'll be more people later on. This place is most popular with families and kids in the middle of the day and on weekends.'

Gracie lifted her dress over her head, and his throat caught. Instead of the neon-yellow T-shirt, she was wearing a one-piece costume in simple black, looking as though it had been painted onto her strong and surprisingly curvy figure.

He swallowed back his reaction, took off his own shirt and followed her toward the water's edge, thinking more about Gracie than his fear of the open water. He tried to push the thoughts aside. She was his teacher. Totally not his type. And not interested in him, anyway. Her cautiousness of celebrities was apparent, her skittishness clear. He and Gracie would never be more than friends.

Yet…

If there was anyone in the world he'd follow into shark-infested waters, it would be Gracie.

She looked back over her shoulder to make sure he wasn't chickening out, and he met her big brown eyes again. So captivating, it took him a moment to realise he was now ankle-deep in water.

Cold water.

He gasped.

'Yes, it's cooler than your pool, but you'll get used to it. Expect another shock at waist height and again at your nipples.'

Gracie was already in up to her waist. The last thing he needed at this point was anyone mentioning nipples.

The sand felt different under his feet than the pool floor, but it was still firm. The water was crystal clear above it. It stretched off into the dark, deep, unknowable harbour, but right here, in the shallows, he could see his feet, and Gracie's too, for that matter. He waded further in. With each step, he felt the cold water anew, but she was right. His breath caught with each step in, but there was an incentive to keep wading. It was three feet in front of him with long brown hair in wavy tresses loose down her back.

Gracie dived into the surf and surfaced ten or so feet away from him. She slicked her hair back from her face, turned to him and smiled again.

'You can do this. It isn't any deeper than the middle of your pool.' She walked backwards further from him. 'Catch me.'

Fear, worry, everything dropped away. He wanted to catch her. Touch her. He was worried— of course he was—but somehow that was less important than following her. Walking at first. Then he lifted his feet up, and he was finally swimming. He had reached her by the time he realised he could no longer touch the ground.

He yelped and immediately forgot all the things she'd told him about treading water.

'Don't panic,' she cautioned, looking him straight in the eye. 'You can do this. You've done this in the pool. If in doubt, what do you do?'

'Float on my back. Relax.'

'So do that.'

He did. The salt water made him surprisingly buoyant. It was easier to float here than in his pool, even with the gentle motion of the water. Gracie was next to him again, only an arm's length away, and that alone made him feel lighter.

'Well done. How are you feeling?'

He thought about his answer. 'Good. I love the way this water feels.' He deliberately wasn't thinking about the sharks. Much.

She took a few more strokes towards the shore. 'Chase me again.'

He turned onto his stomach and did what he'd been practising, one arm after the other. Kicking his feet, he was moving towards her. Not fast, but he was definitely moving in her direction.

In fewer strokes than he'd anticipated, he caught up to her, touching her shoulder ever so lightly and loving the way her smooth skin felt in the water. She laughed and pulled away.

He loved how *he* felt in the water, how the salt water felt on his skin. He loved the sound of her laughter even more.

'You can touch the bottom here,' she said, and he did, planting his feet firmly into the sand, but instantly wanting to lift them again and practice the strokes he'd been learning.

Gracie pointed her arms and took a graceful dive into the water. It was captivating, the way she moved through the water. Her limbs were strong, and her body curved in just the perfect way to slice the water and make it look like air.

'Can you show me how to do that?'

'Sure, if you feel ready?'

He did feel ready. Here on this beach he felt alive. Confident.

She stood next to him and showed him how she pointed her arms, getting him to copy her. He watched her, did as she did, but even though he was waist-deep in the water, he still landed hard on his chest and chin, swallowing a mouthful of seawater in the process.

He pulled himself up sheepishly but she wasn't laughing.

*She never laughs at my mistakes.*

'Here, let me show you.' She stepped behind him and placed her hands on his arms to hold them in the right position.

*Focus on your arms, not on her hands. Or her warm fingertips. And definitely not on her chest brushing against your back and the way you can feel the sensation right up your neck and down to your toes.*

'Do you want to swim out a little further with me? I think you can.'

He wanted to, more than anything. But this was Sydney Harbour, and he'd only been learning for just over a week. Was he ready?

'Not too far,' he said.

'Of course not. Just yell stop when you need to.'

They swam out about twenty feet, and it was Gracie who stopped first. She indicated they should head back, and they turned. Then they swam short laps across the calm waters of the bay. Being in the salt water felt different on his skin. The open water allowed him to stretch himself and practice his strokes.

Gracie was really special. Like no one he'd met in a very long time.

'Thank you for staying on as my teacher,' he said when they were sitting on the beach.

She shrugged. 'Thank you for not being weird when I freaked out.'

'No need to thank me. I'm sure before this is over, I'll freak out at some point as well.'

'Yeah, but not…not like that. You're doing really great. You know that, don't you? You're a very good pupil.'

'No, I just have a very good teacher.'

He smiled at her, and she looked down. But a moment later, she looked back up. Her smile was shy but genuine, and he felt it deep in his chest. For the first time all morning, he felt breathless.

It was a welcome relief to drive to the White Horses pool on Saturday morning for her usual children's classes. Kids were straightforward. Kids didn't send her heart fluttering into her throat or her stomach diving each time they looked at her.

In one more week, her assignment would mostly

be over, along with the drive up to Watsons Bay, and being professionally compelled to not take her eyes from Connor Day and his beautiful body. Being professionally obliged to occasionally touch said beautiful body. Life would go back to normal. How it should be.

Gracie slid into the familiar pool and greeted her young students. First a class of ten-year-olds. Then a class of two-years-olds being held by their parents. When that class ended, one of the fathers winked at her as he said goodbye, which she would have passed off as a random sleazy encounter if one of the mothers hadn't also smiled slyly at her and said, 'Way to go, Gracie.'

What?

When she finished a class of especially rowdy six-year-olds and passed them back to their parents, they also gave her odd looks. She wrapped a towel around herself and headed to the break room, but on the way, Virginia signalled to her from across the pool and pointed her thumb to the office.

She didn't look happy.

Still dripping, Gracie did as she was told.

'What's up?'

'Have you been online this morning?' Virginia asked.

'I checked the weather.'

Virginia shook her head. 'You need to see this.' She stepped to one side so Gracie could view her computer screen. It took her a few beats to realise what—and who—she was looking at. Parsley Bay. Sunrise. Two people frolicking in the water. One of them was Connor.

And of course the other one was her.

'Who's seen this?' Gracie asked.

'Um, everyone in the world except you and probably some Sherpa in Nepal.'

'Everyone?' Her parents? No, probably not her parents, because they rarely used their smart-phones and didn't follow celebrity gossip.

'Everyone that matters. I've just had Bruce, Connor's manager, on the phone. He's furious. Threatening to end the whole deal.'

'That's ridiculous.'

'Secrecy. Discretion. That was the condition, and yet here you are taking him to a public beach!'

No. They couldn't end the deal. Not after she'd spent so long convincing herself to do it. Not when Connor was making such good progress.

'He didn't have a problem with it! He needs to be comfortable with the salt water for his role. Besides, no one knows I'm teaching him. We just look like two friends having a swim.'

'That's the other thing.'

Virginia clicked out of the photograph, reveal-ing a page of search results. Headlines screamed at her. 'Connor Day's new love!' 'Heartthrob ready to announce his new relationship!' 'Connor's Aus-sie girlfriend!'

'What?' she exclaimed. 'That's ridiculous. Why would they assume we're dating?'

'Because it's the media, and because, quite frankly, you two look very close.'

'I was teaching him.'

'But no one is meant to *know* that,' Virginia said.

Aware for the first time that the moisture dripping off her was not pool water but perspiration, Gracie's mouth was dry. She swallowed and wished she had her water bottle. This was all awkward, highly embarrassing. Everyone had seen this and had apparently added two and two together to make fifty million.

'Do they want to end the contract?'

'No, I managed to talk Bruce round. Connor still needs to learn to swim, and he still wants you, but Bruce and the studio are still insisting on discretion. And I still need the money.'

'Good, so we'll just keep going as we are, and Connor and I will be more careful.'

'Not exactly.'

'Bruce will set the story straight? Tell the press we're just friends?' Even as she said it, a lump was forming in her gut.

'No. They're going to lean into it instead.'

'Lean into…what?'

'You're going along with the story that you're a couple.'

Gracie laughed. Hard.

'Yes,' Virginia said right back. 'You have to.'

'No, I don't.'

'It's a term of the contract.'

'Please tell me you didn't sign a new contract saying I'd pretend to be in a relationship with a movie star?' A sentence she'd never imagined herself saying.

'Not exactly. But we agreed you would…' Virginia read out loud from a paper on her desk '"…do everything within your power and ability to maintain the privacy of Mr Day."'

The room felt like it was swaying. 'So?'

'So, in this case, it means you won't disagree with the speculation that you and Connor are a couple, and that's the reason you were at the beach together. First thing in the morning.'

'He needs to learn to swim in the ocean, for the film. I thought…'

Virginia's expression softened. 'Yes, I see. But what's the problem with going along with it? With simply not contradicting the reports that you're a couple?'

'Because it's ridiculous! It's not believable.'

Gracie glanced behind Virginia to the computer screen and the photographs. She crossed her arms. The whole world was currently looking at photos of her in her swimwear. The whole world thought she was sleeping with Connor Day.

She didn't feel excited. She felt exposed. Like an

intruder had ransacked her house and posted photos of her underwear drawer all over the internet.

'Of course it's believable. Visiting movie star meets a local girl, falls for her. What's not believable about that?'

*I'm me. I'm Gracie Sutherland. I rarely divert from the path between my home, my work and my parents' house. My life is simple, and I've spent lots of effort trying to make it so.*

'Can't I be something else? His friend? His cousin?'

Virginia smirked. 'Connor is six foot and then some with the most famous head of blond hair in the world. You're a petite brunette with no genetic connection to him. Cousin is less believable than lover.'

'It could happen. Genetics are a crazy thing.'

Virginia turned back to the screen and clicked on one of the photos. 'Besides, you look good together.'

Gracie scoffed. 'No, we don't.' Something shifted inside her as she looked at the photo. It was a strange perspective to see yourself from. Connor's tall, broad frame towering over her, the smile on his face as he looked down at her.

'You're a good swim instructor. And a great friend. Not to mention a believable girlfriend for Connor Day.'

Gracie shook her head. 'They'll catch on. Besides, Connor won't agree.'

Virginia tilted her head as she said, 'Why would you say that? Actually, don't even answer that. I don't want to hear some pity story that exists only in your head. Connor has already agreed.'

'He…?'

Connor must have been browbeaten into this by Bruce just as Virginia was browbeating her. He wouldn't have agreed without some serious persuading. Or threats. What a mess.

'One more thing. I'm giving you time off from your regular lessons.'

'No!'

'I don't want photographers crawling around here. Spending time with Connor will make it more believable. For the next few weeks, your job description is being Connor Day's girlfriend. And teaching him to swim believably. So I don't want to see you here.'

'But there's only one more week of lessons.'

'And now there are several more. If he can already swim, fine, but your job for the next while is being his girlfriend.'

Gracie sighed.

'It won't hurt you to have a break, do something different. You never know, you might even have fun.'

'I hate you,' Gracie muttered.

'No, you don't.'

Virginia was right. Gracie didn't hate her. She owed Virginia more than she could ever repay.

Years of friendship, of gentle, patient listening. Virginia was the only person Gracie had ever been able to open up to fully about Caroline. Virginia was the only one who understood why Gracie had ended her engagement.

But at this moment, she didn't like anyone very much, and the person at Parsley Bay who had taken those photographs was at the top of her list.

Gracie walked out of Virginia's office, limbs tingling with panic, and made her way around the pool to the change room.

*People are looking at you.*

Some were openly staring. Others kept their posture fixed, but their eyes still moved in her direction.

She finally made it to the change rooms and ensconced herself in a cubicle. Her hands shook as she checked her phone, a falling card deck of notifications, messages and missed calls.

Of course. Everyone had seen the photos. Even her mother wanted to know why Gracie hadn't told her she had a boyfriend and asked when she could meet him. People she didn't know were tagging her in all sorts of things.

The only notification she clicked on was one of the many missed calls from Connor. He picked up right away, but before he could say anything, she said, 'I'm coming right away.'

Gracie was halfway to Connor's house before she realised she hadn't changed. She'd just gotten straight into her car in her damp work clothes. They were clinging to her uncomfortably. She wasn't about to turn around to get changed. She had to shut down this nonsense about a fake relationship as soon as possible.

She couldn't belived that Connor had agreed to this charade. Surely he would see how unbelievable it was for them to be a couple. In no conceivable universe would their paths even cross.

She pressed the buzzer, and the gate opened. Connor was standing at the door when she stopped her car in front of the house.

'Have you spoken to your manager?' she asked, scrambling out of her car.

'Repeatedly,' he said with a sigh. 'You should come in.'

'We can't do this,' she said before she was even over the threshold.

'We have to do this.'

She spun. He couldn't actually think this was a good idea!

'No. It's ridiculous. We should just tell them we're friends.' She followed him down the hallway and into the kitchen.

'Have you seen the photos?' he asked.

She'd glanced at them. They were together having a swim. So what? 'Yes, briefly.'

Connor swiped something on his phone and handed it to her. It took her a moment to focus and realise what she was looking at. 'That's me. Leaving White Horses.'

He nodded.

She was wearing her bright yellow White Horses top. A red-and-blue towel was wrapped around her waist. Gracie looked down at herself. 'This is from today! This is from less than an hour ago! How?'

'Because they're following you. Photographers. People are loving this story.'

'There is no story!'

'They don't know that. They think a famous movie star has fallen in love with a pretty local girl. They think it's great.'

'But it isn't true!' Did he just call her pretty?

'That's not the point. We *need* to go along with it,' Connor said. 'Trust me, it's easier this way.'

Easier? 'For you. Not for me.'

'Yes, for you as well. Think about this. If we deny we're a couple, they'll just continue speculating why we're together. That'll be infinitely worse. It's far better to go along with it. In a week or so, they'll move on to some other unsuspecting celebrity couple and forget about us.'

She clenched her fists in a futile attempt to steady herself. He had a good point, and yet every part of her body was fighting against this. Her stomach, arms, legs, and most of all, her brain. The photos of her were everywhere, and she wanted them erased from every computer screen. She wasn't that carefree woman having an early morning swim with the most beautiful man in the world.

'And there's something else. They know you're a swimming instructor. If we don't tell the world we're a couple, it will be a matter of hours before someone puts everything together and wonders if you've been teaching *me*. I can't let that get out. I just can't. For the sake of my career…for…'

He looked stricken, and it didn't appear he was acting. She felt his fear in her gut.

'Please, Gracie, please do it for me. Do it for White Horses. When filming stops, everything will go back to normal. They'll forget about you, and I'll go home.'

She walked from one end of the spacious kitchen to the other and back again. Virginia wanted her to do it. Virginia *needed* her to do it. Fighting it could just make an already painful situation worse.

'Are you ashamed of me?' he asked.

'No! Why would you think that?'

'Because you seem very opposed to this plan.'

'Because…' Gracie stopped pacing and took a deep breath. 'You don't understand. I live a quiet life. I have a few close friends. My cat. My parents. People say it's a small, boring life, but what's wrong with that if it gets me through? Not everyone in the world is famous. Not everyone wants to be. Most of us just want to get on with our lives the best we can, and this is how I get along with mine.' She crossed her arms.

Connor stepped up to her and put one of his large palms gently on her upper arm. Somehow it felt as though he were lifting her up.

'Gracie, I'll look after you. I'm not going to make you do anything you're not comfortable with, but I honestly do think this is the best and quickest way to make it blow over. It'll just be for a few weeks.'

She stared at him. He actually wanted to do this. Connor Day actually thought that she, Gracie Sutherland, could be his fake girlfriend.

The idea should have given her reassurance, but it somehow confused her more.

'What can I do to make you more comfortable?' he asked.

She shook her head. 'Nothing.' She liked him. She trusted him. She wanted to help him. 'It isn't you. It's the situation.'

He nodded, but she wasn't sure he really did understand. This kind of thing happened to him every day.

'Gracie, this doesn't mean we have to… I'm not expecting you to… This is a fake relationship only.'

Her face burnt. 'Yes, I know. I'm not worried about…that.'

That! A physical relationship. Somehow the thought of *that* didn't bother her at all. It was the deception, the lying and the risk the lie would be found out. It was also that it wouldn't take the rest of the world long to realise what Gracie already knew. Connor didn't belong with someone like her.

The fact that this meant she'd be spending more time with Connor wasn't a problem. In fact, right now, it was the single item in the 'pro' column she was drafting in her head.

'How would you feel about moving in?' he asked.

She blinked. She mustn't have heard him correctly. 'With you? Here?'

He nodded. 'It'll help establish our story. Plus there's more security. I think it would help maintain your privacy. Given the photo from this morning.'

She lowered her head. Just thinking of the photo of her leaving White Horses with her towel still wrapped around her waist made her queasy. 'I would feel safer here. Thank you.'

'Good. I think you will be too. And it'll be nice to have some company.'

She looked back up. Connor was smiling down at her. The sensation in her stomach shifted from unsteadiness to a big ball of air. His hands were still on her arms, still holding her, supporting her. Yes, staying here was the best thing to do.

*Is it? Won't it perhaps be a little too tempting to be around him all the time?* She dismissed that concern with the voice of reason, no matter how tempted she was.

'Can I bring my cat?'

'Of course. There's heaps of room.'

One knot of anxiety unhitched. At least she'd have Biscuit with her.

'And I'll still have to visit my parents.'

'You won't be a prisoner.' He grinned.

But it would probably be best for her parents if she didn't visit their place much until this charade came to its inevitable end.

His phone buzzed, and he let go of her to answer it. She was still in her swimmers and towel, but luckily she'd had the sense to grab her bag when she'd jumped out of the car. She went to one of the spare rooms and changed into dry clothes, some denim shorts and a T-shirt. When she came out, Connor was pacing the kitchen.

'What's happened?'

'Sorry, but now I've just got you feeling relaxed about our new arrangement, there's something else. There's a cast and crew thing tonight.'

'Oh, okay. I can move in tomorrow.'

'No, I mean, you should move in today. You're invited to the party tonight.'

'Oh.'

'But don't worry, it's a private function. No cameras, and everyone there is covered by NDAs,' he said.

'Why?'

'To protect the privacy of the guests.'

'No, I mean, why would I come?'

'As my plus one. My date. And it will be a good, gentle way for you to meet the cast and crew.'

This day was already spinning out of control, and it wasn't even lunchtime. At this rate, she'd be fake married to him by sunset.

'They're all lovely, and most people who work on film sets aren't famous. Remember that.'

'I don't have a fear of famous people!'

*I have a fear of new situations, people I don't know. Stepping outside of my comfort zone. And of photographs of me in my swimsuit being splashed across social media.* Not a phobia the Greeks probably had a name for.

'Great, so you'll come,' he said. 'Why don't I send around a car to get you later this afternoon, and we can go to the thing together?'

She didn't have a choice. It was too late to stop this without throwing herself off a speeding train. Without Connor and his kindness, she wasn't sure what she'd do.

Back in her car, Gracie sent a message to Virginia and asked her if she could water her plants for a week or two. She finally dared to open all her messages and notifications.

There were two more notifications from her mother. The first asking again when she could meet Connor. The second asking why she hadn't responded to the first. Gracie groaned.

There were also messages from her workmates. Some acquaintances she hadn't seen for years.

For crying out loud! It was ridiculous, people she hadn't heard from in forever coming out of the woodwork because of a couple of photos of her and a famous person.

Only then did she click on one of the photos of their morning at Parsley Bay.

They were both lying on their backs, side by side, in the sparkling clear water. She'd been giving him a lesson, and it had been the first time he'd floated in salt water, but the photo simply appeared to show two people relaxing in the harbour as rays of sunlight illuminated them.

They could just be friends.

But then she opened a second photo and zoomed in. She was standing behind him with her hands on his arms, showing him the correct position for a dive. She was teaching him. She knew what had happened, and Connor did, too. But through the lens of someone who didn't know she was teaching him, it appeared she was embracing him from behind. They looked like they were two people who were well acquainted with one another's bodies.

Virginia was right. The only possible story, apart from her being his swimming instructor, was that they were lovers. Friends didn't tend to hold one another as she was holding him.

In another photo, she was standing waist-deep in the water. Her hands were held high, celebrating with Connor because he'd just swum ten metres. She looked happy. He looked jubilant. Friends didn't tend to smile at one another quite like she and Connor were as she held her hands aloft.

Gracie's stomach dropped. He was having fun. They were both having fun. The light just made his eyes look all sappy, and the way his head was tilted…well, that was just the angle of the photo. He wasn't really looking at her adoringly.

Or, and this probably was true, the photos had been manipulated to make it look as though they were in love. To sell more papers and magazines.

That was definitely it.

# CHAPTER FIVE

GRACIE HUGGED A cup of tea and looked at Biscuit.

'You'll like it there. I mean, it isn't home, but it's fancy. There's no cat run, but the place is five times the size of this place, so you'll be fine.'

There was a knock at her door. Connor wasn't due for a few more hours. She was still packing. Enjoying the last hours of her regular life.

She opened the door to Virginia.

'Come with me,' Virginia announced.

'I've got to pack.'

'This is more important.'

'Where?'

'It won't take long. I'll help you pack when we get back.'

Because Gracie would do pretty much anything Virginia asked, as the past week had demonstrated, she followed her friend out to her car.

The 'more important' errand was taking Gracie to Virginia's hair salon.

'Just for a cut,' Virginia said as they climbed out of her car.

'I'm not due for one,' she protested.

'You're always due for one. And I know what you're going to say. "What's wrong with the way I look now?" The answer is, nothing at all. We just want you to look as good as you can. I know you, Grace Anne Sutherland. You'll be flipping out about tonight. Let yourself be *Pretty Woman*ed for a moment.'

'I'm pretty sure that's not a verb.'

'Pretty sure I just made it one. Luce, Lilly, what do you think?' Virginia said to the women at the front counter of the salon.

While the hairstylist combed through her tangled hair, the manicurist picked up Gracie's hands and plonked them in water.

'Manicure,' explained Virginia. 'Don't argue.'

Gracie closed her eyes and let them work on her. She was conserving her energy for worrying about the party that night. The people she'd meet. Movie stars. Actresses. Glamorous actresses, because was there any other kind? Connor's glamorous co-stars the world would be comparing her to, because of course they would.

Maybe he'd fall for one of his co-stars. That always happened, didn't it? Gracie would be the jilted footnote in the story of his life. The thought should have buoyed her, but somehow it didn't. After this was all over, she'd be forever famous for being the jilted party in a relationship that didn't even exist.

Given her luck in life so far, that did seem to track. *Connor will look after you.*

She couldn't expect him to stand by her side all night. He'd have to mingle. These were his work-mates.

'Virginia, how do you cope when you go to work functions with Philip?'

'Alcohol,' she replied.

'Seriously?'

'Seriously, it won't be as bad as you think. They'll all be excited to meet you. It'll go quickly.'

If you'd asked her a week ago, Gracie would have said that Virginia was the person in the world she trusted most. Now she wasn't so sure.

'It's like a fairy tale,' Lily said.

'What? With a curse? A witch? Dead parents? Missing children?'

'No. The type with the happily-ever-after ending.'

'I'm thirty-three years old. I stopped believing in those a long time ago.'

Virginia frowned. 'Why can't you have a happily-ever-after?'

'Because he's Connor Day.'

'So? And you're Gracie Sutherland!'

But Gracie Sutherland didn't deserve to be happy.

Connor looked past Gracie into her house and smiled, but when his gaze fell back on her, he frowned.

Gracie looked beautiful. She always looked beautiful, but now she was dressed up. Her hair was in sleek waves down to her chest, which was shown to particular advantage by the black dress. She wore tiny red heels, the sight of which did something to his insides. She was also, for the first time he recalled, wearing makeup. Her beautiful dark eyes were made even sultrier with black lines and dusty shadows.

'Why did you do this?' His voice was tight.

'I was told to.'

'It wasn't your decision?'

'I was practically kidnapped.'

'Good.'

'Why is that good?' she asked. 'What's wrong with it? Should I get changed?'

At the look of horror on her face, it finally dawned on him. What a jerk. She stood frozen before him, her beautiful face looking as though it was about to erupt in tears.

'No, Gracie, you look amazing. It's only that I hate to think you had to go to this much effort. Please don't get me wrong. You look beautiful. But you were beautiful this morning. And yesterday too.'

She crossed her arms and nodded, clearly not quite convinced.

He stepped into her hallway. 'Are you going to give me the tour?'

'It's a two-bedroom cottage, not a Hollywood mansion.'

'You have a weird idea about what Hollywood actually involves,' he said. *And I'd like to show you what it's really like.* Though he didn't say that last part out loud. Gracie was spooked enough by what was happening to her, and not without reason. He'd counted no fewer than five photographers on her street. It was a good thing he'd come to collect her and that she'd be staying with him. Her life, at least for the next few weeks, was going to be very different from what she was used to.

He walked down a short corridor lined with gorgeous framed photographs of the bush, beaches and birds. To his left was a closed door, to his right a bedroom strewn with clothes and the mess of packing.

'I'm nearly ready. Really. I'm just trying to find Biscuit, but now that you're here, she's run for cover.'

'Biscuit! Biscuit!' he called.

'She's not going to come. She's even shier than I am.'

That was saying something, although Gracie was becoming less skittish as they'd gotten to know one another. Yesterday, at Parsley Bay, she'd been anything but. She'd been playful and flirty, and that fun-loving nature was what the cameras had caught.

He should have been more careful than to go out

in public with her like that, but at this moment in time, he didn't care. He wanted Gracie and Biscuit to come and stay with him. He liked the idea of having a friend around for the next few weeks as he prepared for the hardest role of his life.

At the end of the hallway was a large sunlit room, a kitchen and living area all in one, opening out to an outdoor space. A large cat run looped around a lush garden. There were purple clumps of lavender and hydrangeas, and a hibiscus in full orange bloom. There were also raised beds of vegetables covered in netting. Bees buzzed happily around. It was the prettiest backyard he'd ever seen.

The living room was also filled with greenery, pot plants and ferns. The two couches faced each other, not a television screen, and he had the unmistakable and almost irresistible urge to sink into one. It was a pity they were due at the cast and crew party in under two hours.

He studied the frames mounted on the walls. There were certificates and an award for lifesaving. A medal. He knew she was good at her job, but it warmed his chest to see that she had received the recognition she deserved.

'Biscuit? Biscuit?' he called again. 'Did you know that in America she'd be called Cookie?'

'Cookies are still cookies, but biscuits are different. They're harder. Except in America, where they are scones,' Gracie said as she gathered things into a bag.

He laughed. 'Scone? Cookie?' he called softly and bent down to look for the elusive cat.

'You should wait in the car. She isn't going to come out while you're here.'

A small meow in the hallway made them both spin. A cat, the size of a large kitten, stood pressed against one wall of the hallway but regarded them both.

'Hello, Biscuit. Aren't you beautiful,' crooned Connor. The cat slid slowly but surely to them both, still taking cover against the wall. When Biscuit was close enough, Gracie snatched her up in a swift move.

Connor held out his hand for Biscuit to sniff, which she did. When Biscuit nodded her assent he slid his hand gently under her neck and up to rub her behind the ears. The cat half closed her eyes and purred loudly.

'Shy? Really?'

'With most mortals. I guess your star power strikes again.'

'Ha-ha. Has *she* seen my movies?'

'She doesn't care for them. She prefers Ryan Gosling.'

'Ouch.' He pressed his palm to his chest.

Gracie put a protesting Biscuit into her carrier, and they packed the cat and Gracie's suitcase into the car.

Connor didn't alert Gracie to the photographers waiting outside in their cars but hurried her along nonetheless. Once behind the tinted windows of his car, he turned to her and said, 'I think this is definitely the right decision.'

She nodded.

'I'm not sure if you noticed, but are there more cars in this street than usual.'

Her face turned pale the moment she figured it out. 'Photographers?'

'A couple, yes. It'll be much easier to protect your privacy at my place.'

Gracie hugged herself tight and he started the ignition.

From the passenger seat, Gracie gave suggestions about the best lane to drive in for the first part of the drive, then sat in silence. So much so that he was surprised when about halfway to his house, she said softly, 'The fake relationship thing?'

'Yes.'

'How do you think it'll work?'

'It'll be fine.'

'Fine?' she squeaked.

He knew it was no big deal, but then again, he pretended for a living. Gracie was nothing if not honest. He doubted she'd told a lie in her life. He found he could read the feelings on her face like a neon sign. Almost as bright as her fluorescent yellow rash vest.

'It's nothing to worry about, trust me. I've done it before.'

'You've had a fake relationship with your swim instructor?'

'No, not a swim instructor. But co-stars. Celebrities. Artists. You know.'

She shook her head. 'No. I don't know. This is definitely my first fake relationship. Wait, also, what? You've done this more than once?'

'I have.' He didn't need to take his eyes off the road to know that Gracie's mouth was probably hanging open, aghast.

They drove a little further in silence before she said, 'Well, don't be shy! If we're fake dating, I should know about all your other fake relationships.'

'I can't tell if you're joking,' he said.

'That's because this whole thing is messed up.'

He took a deep breath. 'Sometimes we're asked to fake—or at least not deny—a relationship for publicity purposes. No one ever makes us do anything we don't want to do. It's not like that. It's just…'

'Lying?'

'No. Making room for speculation. Creating a buzz.'

'Alright,' she said in a tone that indicated it was anything but.

'When I landed my first major role, Bruce got

me to go on a few dates with another one of his clients, an actress who was already well established.'

'Stephanie Castle?'

He glanced at Gracie, but her face was impassive. He'd dated Stephanie well over a decade ago and rarely thought of her these days. He was surprised Gracie knew or even remembered. 'Yes.'

'What about Amanda? Was that fake, too?'

Amanda Kim had also been a co-star and was his last long-term relationship. They'd been together for six months.

'Yeah, when we were both cast, we were both single, and the producers told us it wouldn't hurt if we were seen out together. We weren't told to date, per se, but encouraged to spend time together. We hit it off.'

'Wait, have all your relationships started out… as fake?'

'Not all. But I guess some.'

'I knew Hollywood was strange, but seriously?'

'Pretending to be in a relationship is really no big deal. It only gets messy when you have to pretend to be in love with someone when you've already broken up. Making a convincing rom-com with the woman I'd just broken up with is currently my greatest acting achievement. Only I can't put it on my résumé.' He laughed, but she didn't even smile.

'Of course, that won't be a problem for us,' he said quickly.

'Of course not.' She crossed her arms.

That last comment had come out wrong, but he wasn't sure how to explain what he really meant. He wanted to reassure her that he wasn't expecting this relationship to develop into anything more than it was. A professional friendship.

His relationships with Stephanie and Amanda had been different. They were actresses, celebrities who also needed the publicity. Gracie did not want the publicity and had only reluctantly agreed to the ruse.

Besides, Stephanie and Amanda knew the score. They weren't looking for a serious relationship either. Both had been prepared to do anything for their careers, just like Connor.

'We're different. We'll just stay friends. You know that, don't you?' he said.

She gulped and nodded. 'Of course.'

'I mean, we're doing this for entirely different reasons than those I had with Stephanie or Amanda.'

'Yes, this isn't about getting publicity. It's about stopping publicity. It's for Bruce. And Virginia,' she said.

'I feel guilty enough about dragging you into this part of my crazy life. I'm not going to let this get any messier than it already is.'

'I understand. And you've been nothing but kind and understanding. I appreciate that.'

* * *

At his house, Gracie took Biscuit's carrier and Connor carried her suitcase, showing her to the room he'd had made up for her. It was the furthest away in the house from his.

'This is the second largest room, so I thought you might like this one, but feel free to move to any of the others if you think they're more comfortable,' he offered.

'This will be great, thanks.'

She placed the carrier on the carpeted floor of her room and opened the door. Biscuit did not emerge.

'The car is picking us up in about an hour. Do you want something to drink before we go? Wine?'

'I'll take a chance with one of your coffees.'

'Coming right up.'

He went to the kitchen and was surprised when moments later, Gracie was behind him with a meowing Biscuit.

'Where's your laundry? Do you mind if I put her food and litter tray in there?'

He pointed to a door on the left of the kitchen. 'It's through there, and of course. You don't have to ask. I've only lived here about one week longer than you have.'

They sat on the couch, and they drank their coffee. Part of him would have preferred something stiffer before the party, but Gracie was anxious enough about tonight as it was, and he would take his cues from her.

'How does a fake relationship work? I'd like to learn from the expert.'

The way she put it made him slightly queasy. He didn't like lying. It was never his first choice. But sometimes it was necessary. He only lied when it was necessary to protect others.

'It works a lot like any other relationship.'

'I'm pretty sure it doesn't.'

'I mean, it works best with friendship and honesty. Like other relationships.'

'I suppose that's fair.'

'We keep talking. We don't get stressed about little details, because people aren't studying us and looking for signs we're really dating.'

She laughed. 'Nope, not me. From now on, I will assume that every relationship a Hollywood actor is in is fake.'

He shook his head. 'People won't ask anything intrusive. Trust me, they take things at face value. What can I do to make you comfortable?'

She grimaced. 'It's not you, or anything you're doing or not doing. It's the situation.'

'You know me. We're friends, aren't we?'

After a beat too long, she said, 'Yes.'

'Then tell me what I can do. I've put my life in your hands, literally. You can trust me.'

'You weren't going to drown.'

'I know. Because you were always going to save

me. And…' He picked up her hand. 'You can trust that I'm not going to let *you* drown.'

She looked down at their hands clasped together. Warm. Comforting. Grounding.

'There'll be water at this party?'

*No. But there will be sharks.* He couldn't say that and freak her out entirely.

'It's just like any other party.'

'I don't go to a lot of parties.'

'Parties are just talking to people but with louder music. And often alcohol. I won't leave your side.'

She raised a sceptical eyebrow.

'People really aren't going to ask us intimate details about one another. The only question they'll probably ask is how we met.'

'I suppose we can't say I'm your swimming instructor?'

'It's about the only thing we can't say. What about a dating app?'

'You go on dating apps?' she asked.

'Why wouldn't I?'

'You don't need to, for starters.'

'Dating apps can be good for quickly finding out about someone and getting to know them a bit before you meet. Don't you go on the apps?'

She shook her head.

'You manage to meet people in real life?'

'I just don't tend to date.'

He knew she was reserved, but this was still a

surprise. Quite frankly, it was a surprise that some-one as lovely as Gracie wasn't in a relationship.

'Why not? If you don't mind me asking?'

'I'm not looking for a relationship. And one of the good things about not wanting a relationship is that you don't have to date. And you don't have to go on the apps. It's a win-win.'

'Dating is fun.'

She scoffed. 'Oh, sure it is—when you look like you do.'

'No, I like meeting people. I'm interested in people. Dating doesn't always have to be romantic or lead to sex.'

'Okay, so…dating can be platonic.'

'Yes, and we're fake dating platonically.'

'I'm pretty sure all fake relationships are platonic.' She laughed. 'But thank you for being so good about this. I feel like I'm learning from the fake dating expert. One more thing to put on your résumé.'

His gut churned even more. The way she spoke made it all sound so…wrong.

And maybe it was. Gracie had integrity, and he didn't. He was a liar and had always been a liar. A manipulator. Just like his father. He might tell himself that he only lied to be altruistic, but next to Gracie, he wasn't so sure.

*Who are you kidding? You've been a fraud for as long as you can remember. Fooling others is as easy as breathing to you. What else is acting?*

Gracie deserved better, and he resolved to be better for her.

'If not a dating app, then what? In a bar?' he wondered. 'You…just walked up to me…in a bar?'

She laughed. 'It's more believable if I walked up to you. And yet that's also unbelievable.'

'Why? Why do you think everyone will have such a hard time believing we're together?'

'Because I'm me.'

Oh. He remembered all the things he knew about her. Reserved, though passionate about her job. Shy yet strong. Devoted to her parents, even though they let her believe she was responsible for her sister's death. And carrying more unnecessary guilt around than anyone should. And none of those things remotely meant she wasn't worthy of love.

If anyone wasn't worthy of love, it was him. She was far too good for him.

'Gracie, if this is going to work, you're going to have to start thinking you're worthy of me.'

'It's not that I think I'm unworthy. It isn't that at all. It's just that I think we're too…too improbable.'

That, he conceded, was true.

He smiled. 'Then we make up a story as improbable as we are.'

She snorted and put down her empty mug. Biscuit jumped into her lap.

This place was nicer with a pet around. He hadn't had a pet since he'd lived with his mother.

A cat called Sammy. A dog, though. He'd love to have a dog. But nomadic actors did not get to have dogs. Or girlfriends who weren't fake, apparently.

'What kind of improbable?' she asked.

'Oh, you know, something that's so unlikely it makes sense for us.'

She was quiet for so many beats. And then she said, 'Something like we passed in the street, I dropped something, and you stopped to pick it up? But no, we're so improbable we wouldn't even be walking along the same street. We don't have any-thing in common.'

'Keep as close as possible to the truth.'

'What?'

'We stay as close as possible to the truth. The thing we have in common is swimming.'

'But you can't…'

'But the world doesn't know that. So we met swimming.'

'At Parsley Bay?' she asked.

'That's it. Now you've got it.'

'We met at Parsley Bay, as we were both there for a morning swim.'

'And you walked up to me—' he said.

'Hardly! You mean you came up to me!'

'Sure.'

Her face fell. 'Yeah, sorry, that's unlikely as well.'

'No, Gracie.' He touched her forearm. 'Of course I'd approach you.'

'How about an accident?'

'Literally?'

'Yes. How about I backed into your car?'

He couldn't help but laugh. 'Why didn't I back into your car?'

'Because I backed into your car.'

'We backed into each other. And we got out to exchange details, and… I called you up and asked you out. And we kept meeting up at Parsley Bay.'

A slow smile gathered across her face, and it did all make sense.

'Improbable. Just like us,' she said.

# CHAPTER SIX

CONNOR'S DRIVER TOOK them the short distance from his house to the party. In the back seat, next to Connor, she clutched her handbag tightly.

She *had* to do this, but not for the reasons she'd thought. Not because Virginia and Bruce were asking her to, but because when Connor looked into her brown eyes with his deep blue ones, the whole world changed colour. Because she couldn't say no to Connor.

Even though he'd been at pains to tell her that this relationship would remain platonic and never progress to anything more, even though he agreed the pair of them were improbable, even though her head was telling her to pick up Biscuit and leave his house, her body was telling her to stay.

In fact, her body was going to make it impossible to leave. Her bones were temporarily liquid, leaving her just a sack of messy feelings.

Connor wore black trousers and a dark grey shirt. The smell of his aftershave alone was enough to make her heart skip a beat, but mixed with Connor's own scent, it was far more delicious and irresistible.

An exclusive bar had been booked out for the cast and film crew. The sort of place Gracie rarely went. It had an unassuming doorway with a sign that you'd only see if you were looking for it. Connor climbed out of the car first, and once Gracie was out, he took her hand. No doubt making sure she couldn't run away.

Only vaguely aware of her surroundings, she followed Connor down a short hallway and into an intimate space filled with people and noise.

Gracie froze. The first person she saw, the woman standing just inside the doorway, was Giselle Boucher. Connor led—or, more accurately, dragged—Gracie over to her.

'Gracie, this is Giselle. She's playing my wife in the film. Giselle, this is Gracie.'

Giselle, a flawless woman Gracie had seen and loved in countless television shows and movies, turned and smiled broadly at Gracie. Her eyes darted quickly back and forth between Connor and Gracie. Then she stepped up to Gracie, took both her hands in hers and squeezed tight. 'Gracie! It is a pleasure to meet you. I'm so glad you came. I hear you aren't in the business?'

Gracie shook her head.

'My wife will be here in a week or so. She's not in the business either and is always so happy when there are other partners who she says are "normal people".'

Giselle was world famous, but Gracie had had no idea she was married. She didn't know who her wife was.

'You're a local?' Giselle asked.

'Yes.'

'Gracie's a swimming instructor. A very good one,' Connor said, and Giselle's eyes widened. Gracie now understood why it was so important that the world believed she and Connor were a couple. If anyone suspected the real reason for their relationship, the secrecy of the swimming lessons would be at risk.

'Jenny's a high school teacher! You really should meet.'

Giselle Boucher was married to a high school teacher. Gracie couldn't quite make that add up in her head.

'How did you two meet?' Gracie asked as though Giselle wasn't a big star anymore, just a friendly person.

'Through some mutual friends. What about you two? Con's been a bit cagey with the details.'

Con?

She met Connor's gaze and silently screamed, *You do this. I can't!*

He must have got the message, because he said, 'At the beach. I was having an early morning swim and I ran into Gracie. Literally.'

'Ran into her?'

'Yes, I reversed into her car.'

'Oh no!' Giselle exclaimed.

'No, I reversed into you,' Gracie said. Wasn't that the story they'd come up with?

'No, it was my fault.'

'No, it was mine,' she insisted. They had to get this right or someone would figure out the truth.

Giselle cooed, 'You two are adorable.'

Gracie glanced at Connor. He was trying hard not to laugh. She was no actress and must have looked horrified.

But Giselle didn't care. 'I'm so pleased for you both.' She squeezed Gracie's hand again.

Giselle asked Gracie more questions about her job. Gracie wasn't even aware that Connor had left her side until he returned with glasses of champagne. When he gave Giselle her glass, she smiled and winked at him while nodding in Gracie's direction. Gracie sipped her drink and felt some of the apprehension slip away. It was going to be okay. Just like she could sometimes forget Connor was world famous, she found herself doing that with Giselle. They were joined by a man who was introduced as Mike from sound and then a steady stream of people Connor had worked with before or was meeting for the first time. They chatted about the film, but also Sydney and what they had been doing since their arrival. Gracie found it very easy to contribute to that part of the conversation. No one acted as though she didn't belong there. Everyone was friendly and lovely. Despite what Giselle's wife might say, they were 'normal people'.

As they finished their second drinks, Giselle turned to Gracie, grabbed her forearm and said, 'Come outside and meet Gerry.'

'Gerry?'

'Our director.'

Connor added, 'Yes, come and meet him. He's great value.'

Gracie followed them out to a larger room with even more people and music playing loudly.

Giselle held Gracie's forearm, and she was aware Connor was nearby, but she couldn't focus on the people. Flashing lights pulsated around the next room. Red and blue. Gracie's head went light, and the ground might as well have fallen out from underneath her. Her stomach dropped. She was going to throw up. She was going throw up at this exclusive party full of Hollywood celebrities. Or she was going to faint. Probably both. But something, or someone, lifted her up and moved her outside, away from the lights and into fresh air. She was helped gently into a chair.

Once she was seated, breathing the fresh night air and away from the flashing lights, the overwhelming sensation she felt was embarrassment. This was exactly why she didn't go out of her comfort zone.

Connor was next to her, holding her hand and looking concerned.

'I'm fine. You should go back in there,' she said.

'Hardly. I'm going to stay here with you. What happened? You went completely white.'

'Connor, go.' It would be best if he left her for a moment to gather herself. Stupid lights. Stupid trigger. Who had red-and-blue lights in a bar anyway?

'Nonsense. You're my girlfriend.'

She glanced around. They were alone. 'You know I'm not,' she muttered.

'I'm your friend, and I'm going to stay with you. What do you need?'

She took a long while to answer.

'I think I just need to breathe for a while.'

'Do you need food, is that it? A glass of water?'

She knew Connor and knew he wasn't going to leave until she told him.

'I just need not to be near those flashing lights.'

He understood in a beat.

And then, because he seemed to have a never-ending supply of kindness, he said, 'I'm so sorry. I didn't realise.'

'I didn't either. I'd forgotten. It's been years.'

Giselle appeared with a glass of cold water and a worried expression.

'Are you okay? Is she okay?'

'She's fine. The room was just a little too warm for her,' Connor said.

Giselle studied them both and said, 'Understood. I'll be back shortly with some food,' she said. 'I'm a fainter as well. Slight drop in blood sugar levels and I'm down.'

Giselle was sweet and not at all what Gracie had been expecting from the femmes fatales she'd played in several movies.

*You were expecting her to be just like her characters?*

Something like that.

Gracie sipped her water and waved at them both. 'Go back in. I'm okay.'

'I'm not leaving you,' Connor said again.

'Don't come back until you feel a hundred and ten percent,' Giselle instructed. 'Go home if you need to. This party isn't that important.' She said the last part to Connor as much as to Gracie and then left.

They sat together in silence for a while, Gracie sipping her water, Connor his wine, both of them letting the summer evening air warm their skin. One of the men she'd met before came out to the courtyard, bringing a plate full of sushi and mini burgers.

She was touched by everyone's kindness and ate a couple of pieces of sushi. She started to feel almost normal. She still had that gentle thrum in her chest, but that was due to Connor and his aftershave and not the flashing lights.

He turned to her and picked up her hands. Gracie looked down at his large hands encircling hers. He had rolled up his sleeves since leaving home, exposing his strong, tanned forearms.

'Gracie,' he said, and she looked up. The grey colour of his shirt should not have been so flattering, but it made the blue of his eyes sparkle.

*This man is not human.*

'Is there anything else I should know about?' he asked softly.

'What do you mean?'

'Triggers?'

She shook her head. 'No. I mean, I guess considering what's happened in the last week, yes. But usually...'

'Usually you avoid new people and new situations, and you don't do anything that might cause this to happen?'

'If I see blue flashing lights when I'm out and about, I stop and stay clear. I didn't expect them at a bar.'

The day Caroline died was etched on her brain, and many of the things Gracie remembered, she wished she didn't. The two ambulances. Her mother's howling. The hot pavers beside the pool stinging her feet.

But it was blue flashing lights that prompted the feeling of her skull closing in on her brain, then dizziness, nausea.

'Do you want me to ask them to turn off the lights?' he asked finally.

'No. No. I'll be fine. I know they are there. I can prepare myself. It was just the surprise. Let's go and meet Gerry.'

Connor gave her a sceptical look, but she stood and held up her hands. 'I'm fine, really.'

She took a deep breath. Now she knew she was walking into a room with lights that flashed like emergency vehicles, she would be fine. Not great, but at least her knees weren't about to give way. Connor moved after her and slid his arm around her.

*He wants to make sure you don't collapse.*

Besides, it suited the fake relationship ruse. He didn't love the way their bodies fit together like she did. The way even though he was significantly taller than her, she nestled perfectly against him. The way she felt protected, cared for.

They met Gerry and then a few more people. Gracie accepted another glass of champagne, and the embarrassment of earlier began to slip away. She was surprised when a while later, Connor looked down at her and whispered, 'Let's get out of here.'

'Already?'

'Of course. Let them think we can't wait to get each other on our own.'

Her face burnt again.

If only that were as true for him as it was for her.

'Are you sure you're okay?' Connor asked her as he opened the front door to the house.

'Yes, I'm fine,' she said for the umpteenth time. 'Just embarrassed. I enjoyed meeting Giselle. Is she really that lovely, or was it an act?'

Connor laughed. 'No, she really is that lovely. Not all actors are spoilt narcissists.'

'I didn't—' She followed him down the hallway and into the kitchen.

'It's okay. Some of us are, but she's not. Her wife's great, too.'

'She's married to a teacher. I can't get my head around that.'

'Because all movie stars are married to one another?'

'No. I mean, yes.'

'It happens. It's quite common for famous people to marry less famous people. Too much diva energy in one household can be bad for a relationship.'

'How do they…' Gracie decided to change what she was going to say mid-sentence. 'How does *Jenny* cope with being married to a super famous person?'

'Probably she knows that the person on the screen and on social media is not who Giselle really is. It's just her job. Yes, it's a weird job, but it isn't her entire identity.'

'I guess so.'

Connor made it sound so much simpler than it was.

'Do you still think of me as Connor Day, movie

star, every time we speak, or are there moments when you forget and just think of me as ordinary silly Connor who can't swim and makes questionable coffee?'

At some point on the trip home, Connor had unbuttoned the next button on his shirt and untucked the shirt from his trousers. He'd started to look a bit more like the man she knew and less like Mr Movie Star.

She bit back a smile. 'I guess the latter.'

'Good, because sometimes I forget that you're Gracie Sutherland, swim instructor superstar, and see you as just Biscuit's mother and my friend.' He came and stood next to her. His aftershave still swirled around them both. It was the Connor who smelt of chlorine and sunscreen she was most relaxed with. This Connor, out-on-the-town Connor, made her breath hitch and her heart pound in her throat. Particularly when he was standing so close to her she had to tilt her head right back to look him in the eye.

He took a step back so she didn't have to. 'Look at me.' He held out his hands in supplication. 'I'm just a normal person.'

The way his eyes were like a hypnotic ocean or a star-filled sky were anything but normal. The way her blood was rushing through her ears was also very far from ordinary.

She shook her head. 'You're not a normal person, though, are you?'

'Are you saying I'm abnormal?' he asked with a grin.

She was surprised she managed to retort, 'You know very well what I'm saying.' She moved her gaze up and down his body and tried not to focus too closely on everything she saw there.

'Genetics.' He shrugged.

'It's more than just genetics. You're extremely talented.'

'It's possible you're biased.'

'How? I've only just met you, but I *have* seen several of your movies. Having met you, I can see you're nothing like most of the characters you play. Ergo you must be a good actor.'

He scoffed and stepped further back. 'If only that were true.'

'Connor! Please tell me you're not going to give me some sob story about you think you're not talented?'

'Do you want something else to drink?' Connor opened the fridge and took out a bottle of crisp white wine.

'Nice—avoiding the question.'

He unscrewed the bottle with a crack. 'You know why I'm doing this film. It's the first role I've been offered for ages that really requires me to stretch myself. It's my chance to show the world I have some real talent. That I'm not just a toy boy male model who gets roles based on my looks alone.'

Connor didn't look at her, but something happened to his shoulders. The one on his left dropped, or his right lifted. She wasn't sure. Either way, she recognised the pose. It was the one he'd held when he told her why he'd never learnt to swim. He was telling the truth. It wasn't an act.

He was genuinely feeling sorry for himself.

'Connor, what brought all this on?'

He handed her a glass of wine.

'The first read-through is tomorrow afternoon.'

'Ah, of the script?'

He nodded.

'Nerves? Really?' she asked.

'Why not?'

'I guess because you seemed comfortable with everyone there tonight, and you're doing well at the swimming lessons. I don't know.'

'I often doubt myself before a new role, but it's worse this time.'

'Because of the expectations you have of this role? Of yourself?'

'That, and because it'll be difficult. My performance, the swimming. The rest of the cast is amazing. Giselle is one of the most talented actors working at the moment. And Gerry? I've wanted to work with him for so long. I don't want to let any of them down.'

It was obvious to her that Connor was extremely talented, but she knew as well as anyone that sometimes a person had difficulty seeing themselves the same way others did. She was an expert in self-doubt, or so Virginia often told her.

Neither of them had turned the lights on since arriving back, and the kitchen was only illuminated by a light streaming in from the hallway.

'You're very talented. You are a great actor. You're becoming a good swimmer.'

He shook his head.

'You are. Seriously. Are you always this insecure?'

He snorted. 'I don't think so. But this role's different.'

Gracie searched her brain for all the other things the internet said about Connor to try to reassure him, but the first thing she blurted out was, 'And you're a great kisser.'

His eyes widened, and Gracie felt her cheeks burn. She should have mentioned his dancing skills. His comedic timing. Anything but kissing.

He looked as though he was trying not to smile. 'And how do you know that?'

'It's common knowledge. You're the best kisser in the world, apparently.'

'According to who?'

'That's what they say.'

'They? How many people do you think I've kissed?'

She couldn't quite tell if he was amused or genuinely outraged. 'More than I have,' she admitted.

'I'll accept that, but still not nearly enough to make it a fact that I'm the best kisser in the world.'

'I think it's because of the kiss in that film *Sunrise*. With Amanda.'

'Ah, the kiss that launched a thousand memes.'

'That's the one.' Gracie gulped.

'Well, don't believe everything *they* say.'

She'd had more than her usual allocation of wine, and the memory of Connor's arms around her was still so fresh she could practically taste it. She said, 'It did look good.'

'It was meant to. That was the point.'

'I guess you were dating, though, so that probably helped. I bet you couldn't kiss like that with just anyone.'

Connor raised one perfect eyebrow into a perfect question. Her cheeks burnt. She hadn't meant to issue a challenge. Or maybe she had. She took a sip of wine, and so did he.

'You want to find out?'

Even the crickets and cicadas outside fell silent.

Of course she did. Except, no, she didn't. Or did she?

'I guess maybe we should practice. You know, in case at some stage we have to kiss in front of someone for the act,' she suggested.

'Exactly.'

Gracie bit down on her own lip, and Connor stepped up to her. 'The first rule in a good kiss is not to bite your own lip.'

She pressed her lips together, rubbing them back and forth softly and then soothing them with a flick of her tongue. Connor's pupils were now fully dilated, his eyes the colour of midnight.

'And the second rule?' she asked.

'The second rule, which really should be the first, is to make sure the other person wants to kiss you.'

She wanted to kiss him. Desperately. But just because she wanted to kiss him didn't mean it was a good idea.

'A screen kiss, like you would for the cameras. Because we're acting,' she said to clarify that's all she was talking about.

'Of course,' he replied. 'I assumed that was what we meant.'

Good. They were on the same page. A screen kiss, a no consequences, no emotions practice kiss. That was all.

He took her wine from her hand and placed both glasses on the bench. Just as well. Her hands were suddenly slippery with perspiration.

'The third rule?'

'Pay attention to what the other person is telling you. With their words and their body.'

His gaze travelled up and down her. Once. Then twice. The corner of his mouth twitched. He tilted his head forward, not quite a nod. He was thinking about it. About what to do next.

'And rule four, no tongue for a screen kiss?' she guessed.

'That's a myth. A kiss won't look realistic if there isn't any tongue.'

She was going to melt here on his kitchen floor.

Connor picked up her right hand in his left and entwined his fingers with hers.

'I think you're making these rules up as you go along,' she said.

'Not at all. Rule five is, take it slowly. Anticipation is key.'

He moved closer, brushed his body gently against hers, sending her every pore into high alert. Then he leant down, his face nearly touching her neck. Without connecting with her skin, he inhaled, and with his eyes closed, he looked for all the world as though he were swooning.

*He's not, though. He's showing you a screen kiss.*

Gracie stiffened.

'Rule six is, relax,' he murmured.

Relax! There was more chance of her becoming a movie star.

Connor rubbed his thumb against the side of her hand in small circles, and her heart rate did start to stabilise. Not to drop. Just stabilise. Then he slid his free arm around her waist and pulled her closer to him. Flush against him, their bodies finally touching and not just teasing, she was aware of the sensations in her body changing. Thickening, gathering. She felt warmer, supported. Anticipation began to morph into realisation.

'Rule seven is, position.'

'What?'

He let go of her hand and slid his other arm around her. 'May I?' he asked, and she nodded. He could do anything to her he wanted.

He scooped her up and placed her on the bench, so their faces were now level. With a new perspective, she felt bolder.

'Rule eight is, get closer.'

They were already nailing that one. Any closer and they'd already be kissing. Her lungs were full of his scent, his aftershave, the wine and even the tiniest hint of chlorine. Her stomach clenched. She pulled up her skirt slightly, spreading her legs apart so he could move in even closer to her. This was the most intimate position she'd been in with anyone in years.

'Rule nine?' she whispered, throat dry.

'Close your eyes.'

She did as she was told.

Gracie never found out what rule ten was, because by then, Connor's lips were brushing against hers, featherlight at first. Then, as though he felt her relaxing, his touch was firmer, his tongue brushing over her lips, each of them becoming accustomed to the other's taste, movements and shape.

New sensations overtook her in a rush of endorphins. She desperately wanted to be a good pupil as well as a fast learner. When he pushed his hands up her back, she slid her fingers into his hair. When his lips tugged at hers, she let her tongue explore his.

He changed the rhythm, and she forgot the rest of the rules, lost feeling in her toes. Forgot that this wasn't real but a lesson only. Or a challenge? She didn't know, and for a moment, she didn't care. She was kissing Connor Day, and everything they said about him was true.

She widened her legs instinctively, as far as they could go, her dress hitching up even higher, his body inching even closer to hers. The fabric of his trousers rubbed against the bare skin of her inner thighs, and her head swum from yet another un-familiar yet exciting sensation. She wanted every part of him touching every part of her.

Connor didn't stop the kiss suddenly, but she was gradually aware of him pulling away, of the intensity dropping, of the air returning to her lungs and the oxygen to her head.

She was grateful she didn't have to deal with a sudden withdrawal. Instead, it was as though he was waking her up slowly from a beautiful dream.

When the air between them was cold, she finally opened her eyes.

'How did I do?' She was still breathless.

'You? I thought I was the one being given a score. I have a title to defend.'

'I think your title is safe for the time being,' she panted. 'And that Oscar, it's in the bag,' she whispered, almost to herself.

He stepped back, and Gracie scrambled down from the bench, half expecting her knees to give out completely. But she maintained her balance, and Connor reached back for his glass. As though he were completely unflustered, he took a further sip of wine.

No amount of wine in the world was going to help calm Gracie's nerves after that kiss. It was one thing to understand in theory that Connor was a good kisser, but to get a personal performance…

*Imagine how it would feel if he actually cared about you? If that kiss were real and not just a demonstration?*

Just as well that wasn't something she was going to have to cope with. He was now on the other side of the room as though he couldn't get away from her fast enough.

'You're going to be fine,' she said. 'With the role, that is.' There mustn't be any misunderstanding that she thought their kiss was any more than it was.

'Thanks for the pep talk,' he mumbled, clearly knowing that kissing one another had been a mistake.

'I'd better let you get to bed,' she said. 'You've got a big day tomorrow.'

He nodded, downed the rest of his wine in one go and went to his room.

Gracie stood in the kitchen, lost, confused. The sound of a meow made her look down. Biscuit circled between her legs.

'What are we doing here?' Gracie whispered.

While Connor went to the read-through, Gracie stayed at his enormous house, twiddling her thumbs. She played with Biscuit, read for a while, even picked up the phone to video call her mother.

'What do you think will happen when he finishes filming?' Sharon Sutherland asked.

'We'll probably break up,' Gracie replied. Then her contractual obligations would come to an end, and there would no longer be a need to pretend to be a couple. There wasn't actually anything going on between them.

The kiss last night didn't count. It wasn't a real kiss after all. Just a practice kiss. And so she could prove to Connor that he really was a talented actor.

'But why? You could go to America with him.'

'You know I can't do that.'

'Why not?'

'Because my life is here.'

'Your life can be anywhere. Like with Matt.'

'Don't bring Matt into this. It's nothing to do with him.' Her parents still didn't understand why Gracie had called off her engagement, and nothing she said could get them to understand. Some days she didn't understand it herself. Matt was a lovely man, and he had loved Gracie deeply. But it hadn't been enough. She couldn't live the big, adventurous life he'd wanted them to.

'Besides, you and I both know it won't last.'

Her mother frowned but didn't contradict her.

Everyone at the party last night believed they were a couple. The media thought they were a couple. Even Connor thought they made a believable couple, yet her mother also assumed it would end.

Sharon Sutherland had been a caring, loving mother, but things had changed since the accident. Sharon had never blamed Gracie outright—neither of her parents had—but they didn't have to say anything directly for Gracie to know that they both held Gracie partly responsible for Caroline's death.

They had all been changed by the accident, but it had affected Sharon's ability to cope with many of life's everyday challenges, so Gracie had stepped up. Her father seemed to fare better, at least for a while, after they moved to Sydney, but instead of coping better as the years went on, they seemed to struggle more.

When Gracie began working at White Horses, Virginia had encouraged her to move out of home and into a flat with her. When Virginia had met Philip and moved in with him, Gracie had contemplated moving back in with her parents, but Virginia had persuaded her to get her own place.

'They're already very dependent on you. Maintaining your independence will be best for you all.'

'They need me,' Gracie had told Virginia.

'Your mother might be happier if she learnt to focus less on herself and more on those she purports to love.'

'She's experienced a great tragedy,' Gracie said.

'And so have you!' Virginia replied.

But Virginia didn't understand, not really. Virginia was the only person in the world Gracie had talked to at any length about Caroline, but Virginia still didn't get it completely. Telling her not to feel guilty was meaningless.

'Will we meet him?'

Gracie held back a groan. 'He's not here for long and is very busy with filming, so probably not. Mum, you and I both know it won't last.'

Sharon was silent for a long time before she said, 'You're allowed to be happy, Gracie. You're allowed to let yourself be happy.'

Gracie did sigh now. Her mother had it all wrong. She wished she had the sort of relationship with her mother where she could say, *Mum, it's not a real relationship. It's all for show.* But she didn't, and she couldn't trust her mother not to tell anyone else, so she simply said, 'It really isn't that serious between us. It's just casual. It's nothing to get excited about.'

'Oh, Gracie, of course he won't be serious about

you if you say things like that and talk yourself down.'

She had no idea how to respond to that, so she told her mother there was someone at the door and ended the call.

She thought about going for a walk, but Connor had warned her that a few photographers were camped out near the front of the house, so she just sat by the pool with her book, a rare thing for her, and enjoyed the spectacular view.

A beautiful fortress, she thought.

Connor had a housekeeper, Leanne, who cleaned the house and filled the fridge with fresh, healthy meals and basically did anything he needed, so there wasn't even any housekeeping or meal planning to distract her.

She checked her emails and messaged Virginia with an update, mentioning the panic attack but not the kiss. Then she scrolled through social media. Gracie kept her accounts private but had thousands of notifications that she'd been tagged in posts. She opened them with trepidation, expecting the worst.

Gradually, as she scrolled through, she saw they weren't hostile but friendly. Excited. They were using the hashtag #conderella, which puzzled her at first, until she realised it was a portmanteau of Connor and Cinderella. She had a hashtag.

White Horses also had hundreds more followers. No, thousands.

Some people wanted followers, Virginia for

starters. She was often talking of building their brand. Gracie thought about this for a while. Instead of being afraid, could she treat this as an opportunity? In a few short weeks Connor would be gone. This was her fifteen minutes, her chance to do something with the profile they had. But what?

When Connor arrived back in the early evening, her heart dropped. He did not look like someone who'd nailed a read-through. 'How did it go?' she asked with trepidation.

He shrugged. 'I wasn't the worst person there.'

'It's just a read-through. It's not the real thing, is it?' What was she saying? She had no idea what happened at a read-through or what was expected of someone at one.

Leanne had left some salads and a lasagne that Connor heated up. Gracie lay the table outside, and they ate with the harbour as a backdrop.

He was quiet, and she had run out of things to say.

This house was suffocating. She didn't want to be home, exactly, not knowing that photographers were waiting to snap her leaving the White Horses pool and her house.

But she had to be doing something. She couldn't sit here all day doing nothing.

She should be teaching Connor to swim. As soon as he was strong in the water, she could slip back quietly into her old life.

'Do you have to go back tomorrow?' she asked.

'We probably need to figure out a way to fit in your lessons now things are getting busier for you.'

'No, I have a rehearsal next Wednesday, but nothing before then. I'm all yours.'

*All yours.*

*I suppose it'll end when he goes back to LA.*

'I was thinking it would be good to give you some more practice in the surf. Parsley Bay doesn't have proper surf. You're doing really well in the pool, but I think you need to feel the waves in the ocean.'

'I agree. Where should we go?'

'Anywhere in Sydney might be tricky. Too many people, and you don't need to deal with onlookers as well as everything else.'

'Nor do you,' he said.

'We should go somewhere more secluded. Slightly off the beaten track.'

'Where do you think?'

'Do you mind going for a drive?'

# CHAPTER SEVEN

Cave Beach was like nowhere else Connor had seen before. The drive from Sydney to the South Coast took around three hours. They'd left just before dawn, and he'd checked they weren't being followed by opportunistic photographers lurking outside his house.

Lately he'd found himself relaxing in Gracie's company and had to keep reminding himself that in public, they had to make sure they did nothing to raise questions about the true nature of their relationship. He'd protected his secrets for so many years.

He was close to being able to swim without his mother or anyone else ever having to know the truth. He'd be able to put it all behind him. He wasn't sure why exactly, only that it would be over. That they would all somehow be safe.

They took his hire car and shared the driving, first through Sydney's suburbs, then along a spectacular escarpment, past coastal towns, through the bush, and finally to a national park, a walk past a colony of docile kangaroos, over a sand dune, to this.

The beach was worthy of a starring role in a movie. On one side, a wall of rock sheltered the beach. Below them, a vast expanse of white sand stretched out to a long sweep of rolling waves. It was a bright day with a gentle breeze that created a slight haze of sea spray.

He'd seen some beautiful things already that morning, yet none quite enough to erase the memory of the scorching kiss he and Gracie had shared two nights ago. Flirty, unstoppable and then confusing. Had he been acting? Instructing? It had started as a perverse way of him proving to her that he wasn't a better kisser than any other person. Then it became a sort of lesson, but by the time they'd pulled slowly and uncertainly apart, he felt as though he'd been taught a thing or two. If it had been an amazing kiss, it was as much to do with Gracie as him.

When he'd ended the kiss, she wouldn't meet his eye, so he'd resolved to never let it happen again. She might have been practicing in case they had to kiss in public, but at some point he knew, for him, it risked becoming the real thing.

He was her pupil, her friend, and he needed her to keep his secret. He couldn't risk complicating things, and yet...

*Things are already complicated. You couldn't concentrate at the read-through yesterday. Your head isn't where it is meant to be. You need to get into the state of mind of a grieving father. Not a boy with an impossible crush.*

Gracie must have taken his hesitation for anxiety, because she touched him gently on the arm. Physical touch came easily to them now. They were accustomed to touching one another in the pool. It naturally flowed over into the rest of their relationship. Yet each time she made contact with him, however chaste, however innocent, it was as though he'd been set alight.

'Are you okay? It's not as daunting as it might look.'

'Fine.' He nodded and set off down the dune. The path to the beach was steep and sandy, and more than once, he thought one of them might lose their footing. She took the last few steps, ended in a leap, and landed on the beach with a laugh that echoed around her and in his chest.

'Remember, the waves will be a lot stronger than they were at Parsley Bay.'

He could tell that just by looking at the foam, seeing the sea spray misting in the air and the roar of the waves in his ears.

There were only a few other people at the large beach. It was a quiet weekday morning late in the summer, but she steered him a good distance from the others. At Gracie's suggestion, he wore a black rashie, as she insisted on calling it, and a water-resistant hat to avoid the sun and the stares of onlookers. Gracie also wore a black top and not the neon-yellow one she usually did.

But being recognised wasn't his main worry right now.

*The sixth rule of kissing is, relax.*

'We'll take it slowly,' she said as they began to wade out.

He'd never ventured more than knee-deep in open ocean like this before. But now he'd swum in the pool, and he'd even managed some laps. He knew how to tread water, float on his back. He'd swum in a sheltered cove off Sydney Harbour. But the push and pull of the ocean was something else entirely.

'We're lucky. Late summer is the best time of year for the ocean because the water is at its warmest.' She was making small talk to relax him, he was certain. The first stretch was easy. The water lapping around his ankles was not unlike Parsley Bay. Slowly, gently, Gracie led the way deeper into the water. By the time the water came up to her thighs, it was barely to his knees. With each metre they moved forward, he felt less stable. Each time a wave came through, he braced himself. But after ten minutes or so, he realised he was still standing and was now waist-deep in the water. She turned to him and slipped her arm around his waist, but if the gesture was intended to calm him, it did the opposite. Desire, nearly as strong as the waves, washed through him.

'If anyone recognises us, they'll just think we're swimming together, not that I'm teaching you,' she said.

He nodded. Gracie was being sensible. He was the only one wishing the gesture was more than platonic.

They stood, still holding one another, waiting for the next wave to roll in. It did with more force than the previous ones, but he maintained his balance.

She talked to him about the rocks to the side of the beach, the cave after which the beach was named. He knew he wasn't required to answer, that she was making him feel comfortable as they moved at a snail's pace into the water, becoming accustomed to everything. The temperature, the force of the waves, the way the waves pushed him to the shore and the undertow pulled him out again.

Before he knew it, he felt the cold of the water around his groin, and he gasped. The water was now to his waist. The next large wave hit his nipples with a shock just as great.

She giggled. 'Welcome to the ocean. You'll warm up in a moment.'

Like she promised, in a few more minutes, he didn't notice the temperature. He was only aware of how refreshing the salt water felt on his skin.

'Do you want to try lifting your feet and swimming a few strokes?'

Instinctively he gripped her tighter.

'It's okay. You can stand here. But I know you can do it.'

It was her last words that did it: *I know you can do it*. He wanted to prove her right. Show her that her confidence in him wasn't misplaced.

'We'll do it like before. Swim to me.' Gracie let go of him, fell onto her back and took a few strokes away from him, not taking her eyes off him. Just like in Parsley Bay, moving back to Gracie, who looked so beautiful floating in the water, was an invitation he couldn't refuse.

Unlike in Parsley Bay, she let him catch her. In three strokes, his fingers touched her shoulder. He dropped his feet, momentarily shocked by how much deeper the water was, almost to his chest.

'Okay?' she asked, her wide eyes no doubt mirroring his surprise.

'Yes,' he replied, but when he saw the foam barrelling down at them, he grabbed for her hand.

'Turn around,' she said, and he did. The wave hit them both, but he remained standing.

'I know you feel as though it is deep here, but we should move to just beyond where the waves are breaking. In a moment, another wave will come. For a second, you will be out of your depth. You should relax, jump up and let it lift you. It'll be fine.'

He did as he was told, and his heart skipped a quick beat at the size of the wave coming towards him, but he jumped when Gracie did. She was right. The wave lifted him as he jumped. It was almost like gravity didn't exist. He laughed as his feet hit the sand again.

'Good?' she asked.

'Yes!' An understatement. For a second it was like he was weightless. Combined with the sensation Gracie's smile caused in his chest, he felt amazing.

They practised just jumping over the unbroken waves for a while. He loved the way the water made him feel so weightless, how Gracie's laughter filled his heart. Then she said, 'Next step is to dive into one.'

'Into one?' It was one thing to jump over a wave, but into it?

'Start by closing your eyes and ducking under one, just to get used to it.'

He did as he was told, becoming more and more comfortable with the tug and tow of the water. Though that also might have been the fact that Gracie's sparkling eyes were always there to greet him when he came back up.

And he wanted to see that smile. 'Okay, I'm going into this one.'

He leant forward into an oncoming wave and was picked up and shaken around like he'd been stuck in a washing machine. He struggled to find the surface, or even the ocean floor, and couldn't. Just as panic started to creep in, he felt a strong hand on his arm, and the wave washed away. He was standing again, but coughing and spluttering. Gracie held his torso, but if her intention was to keep him grounded and secure, it had almost the opposite effect. He wanted to pull her to him. Lift her, have her wrap her legs around him, just like she had in the kitchen the other night. He wanted her wrapped around him, small, strong, unstoppable. Insatiable.

'Whoops,' she panted. 'Are you okay?'

He nodded through the coughs. Snot was probably coming out of his nose.

'It happens sometimes. Even occasionally to me. The thing to remember about the surf is that it's unpredictable. Even the most experienced swimmers get knocked over or surprised.'

He took a few more breaths and felt his confidence return, but that might have had something to do with the fact that Gracie's arm was still around his waist. Her body still pressed against his, smooth and lithe and sliding against his in the most delicious way.

'Do you want to go back in?' She nodded towards the beach.

'No, I'd like to try again.' *I want to stay here. With you.*

On his next attempt, Connor hit the water smoothly and took a few strokes under the wave. The water pushed him in the direction of the beach, but his strokes were strong enough to allow him to maintain his position. When he surfaced, Gracie was still next to him, beaming. He couldn't remember the last time he felt so pleased with himself.

They waited for each wave to come, letting the swell lift them up and over it. His body had never felt so light.

'Weightless,' he said mostly to himself. 'I can finally see why people love it so much.'

She smiled at him. 'I love the feeling when I catch a wave, but I love this more. Just bobbing up and down, letting each wave lift me up. It's relaxing. Almost hypnotising.'

*You're hypnotising.*

'We could stay here all day, but how about some lunch? Then maybe try another beach?'

'I can't imagine anywhere more spectacular than this.'

'Then do I have the place for you.'

'They say it has the whitest sand in the world,' Gracie said as they parked and got out of the car.

He could believe it. Hyams Beach was smaller than Cave Beach and less isolated, next to a picturesque village with the same name. He felt instantly at home at the pretty beach with its view across a large bay and its whiter than white sand.

They ate lunch on the balcony of a cafe overlooking the beach, and she explained to him about rips, and signs to look out for that the water was dangerous.

'Sharks?' he asked.

'Americans are obsessed with sharks. They're out there, but the helicopters look for them at this time of the year. You'd have to be very unlucky.'

'Maybe I am.'

She pulled a face. 'You? Unlucky?'

'Why not?'

She raised an eyebrow.

'Because I'm *famous*?' He whispered the final word. They both wore sunglasses, and the other patrons at the cafe seemed oblivious to their presence.

'No, because look at you. And you're talented, successful.'

'Because of genetics.'

'No, Connor! Because of who you are. There are plenty of good-looking people in the world, but not all of them manage to do what you've done with your life.'

Objectively, he knew she was right. But he couldn't get the message to sink in. Next week they would start filming, and even though he was feeling a bit better about his swimming ability, he was far less confident about his ability to perform next to his talented co-stars.

'Are you still feeling nervous about the role?'

He wanted to talk to her about this, was so close to doing so at several points, but then he remembered what Gracie had gone through with her sister. He wondered what had happened the day she died. What Gracie had felt that day and since.

Every time he said his lines, Gracie was in his head.

*Who are you kidding? Gracie's taken up residence in your brain just like she has in your house. You'd be thinking of her no matter what.*

But thinking about ten-year-old Gracie trying and failing to save her sister kept creeping up on him. She lived with that tragedy every day of her life. It had shaped her entire life, and it broke his heart.

'Yes, but no more than usual,' he finally said.

She looked at him as though she knew he was lying but didn't press further.

She needed to find a way to deal with her guilt and trauma, he thought.

*Since you're such an expert in dealing with your childhood issues?*

The script was beautifully written and had so many layers. It was easy playing Jasper Dangerfield. That character didn't have the complexity or layers this character did. He knew Giselle's character's arc was one of forgiveness. But his? He wasn't yet sure. The script didn't give him much to play with. There were no wise lines, no clear ways of conveying that his character would be okay in the end. That he was forgiven. That he had forgiven himself. He had to find a way to convey that to the audience without words.

She mopped up burger sauce with one of her fries.

'This isn't just any role. Giselle, she's won an Oscar. Who wouldn't be intimidated?'

Gracie nodded. 'I get it. I've doubted my ability to do my job as well.'

'You have?'

'Yes. It's hardly the same thing, but I've had students who have been particularly challenging.'

'Me?'

She laughed. 'Egotistical much? No, you're a very good student. The circus you've brought with you is something else, but you're very good.'

He felt as though he'd just won an award.

'Tell me about the others,' he said.

They ate their lunch, and she told him about some of her students, people who had been injured in accidents and needed to relearn how to swim, children with social needs. People with a crippling fear of the water who nevertheless were determined to learn. Gracie Sutherland was amazing. Sitting with her, talking, took his mind off everything.

After lunch and a walk around the headland and the nearby bush, they went for another swim. This time the waves were less intense than they had been at Cave Beach, and the water was crystal clear.

'I know you don't want to hear about sharks, but how do you feel about fish?'

'What?'

'Look down.'

He did and saw a fish the size of a large goldfish swimming past.

'Woah. What is it?'

'There's whiting. And bream. Yellowtail. I can't tell exactly. They're pretty small.'

Once he knew where to look, he noticed others, all sizes. Some as large as his hands. Then his feet. And he was swimming in the water with them. It was incredible. Even a week ago, he wouldn't have imagined he'd be confident enough to do this.

'Look out!' Gracie said as a particularly high wave came towards them. They both jumped at the same time, though she had considerably higher to jump than he did. When the swell passed, his feet were on the sand but Gracie was still floating. He reached for her. The next thing he knew, her legs were against him. He pulled her closer, and her legs wrapped around his waist.

This.

The sensation of a weightless and wet Gracie wrapped around him was almost too much. And at the same time, it wasn't nearly enough.

His body reacted as it had the other night, becoming tight in some places, loose in others, his body threatening to overrule his thoughts. His thoughts forgetting why holding her like this against him wasn't a good idea.

He was only too aware that Gracie hadn't pulled away, that she was looking at him. Their faces were irresistibly level. Her eyes were wide, and her mouth was open. Their arms and torsos were covered with the fabric of their tops. The sensation of her chest pressing against his was distracting enough, but the part of him he noticed the most, the part all the blood in his body was rushing to, was his hands, which were supporting her bare thighs, which were wrapped around his waist. Silken, strong and impossible to forget.

'Are you okay?' she whispered.

He reluctantly nodded. His feet were on solid ground. How could he not be?

Gracie untangled herself and kicked away. It was awful, but he wished for a freak wave to swamp him again so she could rescue him. Touch him. Hold him. So he could feel her body slide up and down his, the salt water pushing them together, then pulling them apart. Over and over.

He had to rein these feeling in. Crush them entirely.

Gracie wasn't like Amanda or the others. She was a wonderful person, and she didn't deserve the chaos he brought with him.

*Your circus.*

That's what she'd called it, and she'd been right. The last time he'd dated a non-celebrity, it had gone badly. She'd hated the public intrusion into his life and consequently into hers. It had ended disastrously for both of them. Never again.

They came out of the water, and she flopped onto the beach.

'You've done great today. You must be exhausted.'

'I am. But in a good way.' In a way he hadn't felt in years. His limbs were sore, but his head and heart felt alive. And his body was humming, still vibrating with the memory of Gracie wrapped around him.

'We'd better think about driving back.'

'You know I don't need to be in Sydney until Friday morning. We could stay the night,' he suggested.

When she didn't answer right away, he scrambled for a further explanation. 'Somewhere near here. We're both exhausted, and I could get more swimming practice in tomorrow.'

'I think that's a good idea. I don't have any clothes, though.'

'I'm sure we can find a shop open somewhere.'

He didn't care what she wore, as long as she was next to him. As long as they could keep doing this.

'What about Biscuit?'

'I can ask Leanne to feed her and check on her. Would you feel comfortable with that?'

It took Gracie a long beat to reply. 'She did take a shine to Leanne.'

'So that's a yes?'

* * *

Gracie walked out of the small boutique with her purchases—a new T-shirt, underwear and a linen dress. Virginia's voice rang in her ears: *'Do something different. You might even have fun.'*

Connor looked up at her from his phone and grimaced.

'What?'

'I asked my assistant to arrange a hotel for us.'

That was the plan. 'And?'

'They have. At the Sapphire.'

She sucked in a breath. That was the most luxurious hotel nearby. The hotel and its adjoining restaurant were the most renowned on this part of the coast.

'They've booked one room.'

Gracie instantly saw the problem. 'Oh. Of course. Everyone thinks we're together.'

Gracie hadn't thought of this either when she'd agreed they stay. She hadn't thought of much except that she didn't want this day with Connor to end. She hadn't even thought of poor Biscuit right away. Practically the only thing on her mind was the memory of Connor lifting her in the waves and her legs wrapping themselves instinctively around his waist, just as they had the other night on the kitchen bench.

'We didn't think this through,' he said.

'We can go back,' she offered.

'You're tired. We both are.'

He was right. The thought of getting into the car and driving all the way back to Sydney didn't appeal. And Connor really would benefit from more time practicing his strokes in the ocean.

'It's okay,' she said. She'd committed. They'd already called Leanne, who was only too happy to spend the night and look after Biscuit. Gracie had her bag of new clothes in her arms and saw that Connor held one too.

They could be mature about this, couldn't they?

'I'm okay with it, if you are?'

'I don't mind,' he said.

Was he being equivocal, or did he not want to pressure her? She couldn't tell. The thought of sharing a bed with Connor was one part terrifying three parts exciting.

*It's no big deal. You're an adult. He is, too. He's not suggesting you sleep together, only that you don't do anything to jeopardise the story you're spinning to the world. Besides, it's not as though you haven't seen him half naked. Or touched him.*

*Or kissed him...*

*Try something different. You might even have fun.*

'I'm okay,' she said.

Connor's assistant had excelled. The room was beautiful with a panoramic view of the bay. And the bed? It wasn't the widest she'd ever seen.

*You're not large. It will be fine.*

'Shower and dinner?' she asked, keeping her voice as casual as she could.

'Definitely,' he said. 'You go first.'

She was bone-tired from the water and the sun. Connor would be even more exhausted, and sleep would be at the forefront of his mind.

There was no need for her to be preoccupied by the anticipation that was building in her belly. They would both fall asleep quickly. She showered and washed her hair. The dress she'd purchased was long on her, as all dresses were, falling to her ankles. But it fit perfectly over her shoulders and bust. She dried off her hair, still wavy with the salt from the water. She swiped a lick of lipstick she found in her handbag over her lips, took a deep breath and walked back into the room.

Connor gulped when he saw her, but she chose to read nothing into it. She sat on the bed, and as she waited for him to shower, she sent Virginia a message. She needed someone else to know about this escapade, but she made it sound like professional courtesy.

In case you hear from anyone else, I wanted to give you a heads up that Connor and I have come down to Jervis Bay and have decided to stay the night, but rest assured we're keeping up appearances by sharing a room.

Gracie put down her phone and listened to the

sounds coming from the bathroom. Running water. Then silence. Some movement. The sounds of Connor drying himself off. Getting dressed. She tried to keep her breathing even. It wasn't as though she wasn't familiar with his body. She'd spent the past few weeks looking at it, giving him tips and pointers on how he was holding it, moving it. So the fact that tonight she'd sleep next to that body and the man inside? It was nothing. Completely normal. Besides, Connor was a professional. She had to be as well. This was all just part of her assignment.

He emerged from the steamy bathroom wearing a fresh shirt. His hair was clean, if slightly ruffled. He looked edible.

They didn't have a booking at the restaurant, but after the waiter took one look at Connor, they were led to the best table in the place, in a corner, but next to the full-length window overlooking the bay.

As they walked to their table, Gracie was aware of the wave of silence that followed them across the room. He squeezed her hand again. *They're looking at him. Not you.*

Connor pulled out a chair for her. He took the seat facing the window, with his back to the room.

'Is it always like that?' she whispered.

'People looking at me and pretending they aren't? Pretty much.'

'I'm sorry,' she said. She couldn't think of anything worse.

'Why are you sorry? I'm the one who brought

you out. We should have got room service. I guess I'd hoped that there might be a corner of the world left where I'm not recognised.'

'There might be, but this isn't it.'

'Next time I'll book us a place high in the Andes. Or deep in the Pyrenees.' He smiled, and Gracie's chest warmed.

Next time?

'Do you want to leave?' he asked.

She shook her head. 'Not at all. I've forgotten them already.'

It wasn't quite the truth, but she was determined to make it so. This was their time together, and who cared about the rest of the world?

He picked up her hand again, and her heart tumbled in her chest.

What was going on here? Was the gesture for their audience, or was it something more? What was real and what wasn't? Her head didn't know, but her body had some very firm opinions on the matter.

It wanted Connor Day. Too bad that wasn't allowed to happen.

When she was on her second glass of wine, she decided that the only way to dampen the tingling sensation that had set up home inside her was to remind herself Connor's last fake relationship hadn't ended well. 'Can I ask you a personal question?'

He went still. 'Of course.'

'Why did you and Amanda break up?'

He chuckled. 'I'm not sure it'll reflect well on me.'

She shook her head. 'That was impertinent of me. You don't have to answer it. After all, we don't really know one another. We have a professional arrangement.'

Even though it involved them being half dressed around one another and pretending they were a couple, it was still a business arrangement.

Connor leant across the table and took her hand. 'It's fine, really. This…deal we have…it isn't like any other.'

Like hand-holding. Gazing into one another's eyes. Like they were doing now. Was it any wonder she didn't know where the line was? Or whether she was about to cross it?

'Amanda said I was too secretive.'

That wasn't what she was expecting. Infidelity. Pressure of work.

'You kept things from her? Or lied to her?'

'She thought I did.'

'And did you?'

'I never lied to her or anything like that.'

'But?'

'Why do you assume there's a but?'

She didn't need to respond. She just looked at him.

'There are some things I feel like talking about and other things I don't.'

He was suddenly closed off. Cagey. Or protective? She hadn't got this sense from Connor before, but then, they weren't in a relationship. She had no reason to know his inner thoughts.

'Sharing personal stuff is probably part of being in a relationship,' she said.

'Probably,' he said. 'No, it definitely is. And I'm not that kind of person. Sharing things doesn't come easy to me.'

She stared at her dinner, wishing she hadn't thought this was a good topic of conversation.

'So, what about you?' he asked, leaning across the table again and speaking softly.

She shook her head. 'I guess I did just ask you to spill your guts.'

He gave her a lopsided grin. 'Kind of. But this isn't a tit for tat deal. You don't have to tell me anything.'

'There's nothing much to tell.'

'You've never been married?'

She laughed.

'Never come close?'

She opened her mouth to deny it but couldn't lie. He gave her a quizzical look.

'Once. A long time ago. It didn't work out.'

'I'm sorry,' he said.

'Don't be. It was for the best.'

'You ended it?'

His comment surprised her. Most people assumed Matt had been the one to call off their engagement, but not Connor.

'Yes.'

'He was a dirtbag?'

She smiled sadly. 'If only. No. He was…*is* a nice guy. I ended it when I realised I couldn't do it.'

'Do what?'

'Give him everything he wanted, be everything he wanted.'

Connor pulled a face. 'Was he giving you everything? Was he good to you?'

'Yes, but the point is, I wasn't right for him. He had a big, exciting life planned for us. He wanted to travel. Possibly live overseas. See the world, and I… I couldn't do it.'

'You're not a traveller?'

She shrugged. She didn't know. What she did know was that the thought of leaving home for any length of time gave her a sick feeling in her stomach.

'My life is here. My parents, my job. He didn't feel as tied down as I am.'

*You can't keep living your life around your parents'*, Virginia had told her.

But breaking off her engagement had nothing to do with her parents. No matter what Virginia had implied.

'It probably wasn't meant to be. Do you regret it?' he asked.

She shook her head. 'I don't. I feel relief. I don't think about him, to be honest.'

'I'm sure it was the right decision.'

'It was,' she said. 'He met someone else. They've got two kids now. I'm happy for him.'

*And I'm happy too. I have everything I need. My life is quiet, under control. Safe.*

At least it had been until Connor came along.

His body was alive with a strange mix of exhaustion and exhilaration. They had left Sydney in the dark that very morning, but that seemed like days ago, so much had happened since. As he lay in the bed next to Gracie, his limbs were sore, but his body was on fire. After the amazing but exhausting day in the surf, Connor hadn't expected to feel even more churned up after dinner—or after Gracie's revelation she had once been engaged.

He also hadn't expected to open up about Amanda and the end of their relationship, but he knew he could trust Gracie with the truth. He'd been honest with her about one of his deepest secrets—his inability to swim—and she had helped without thinking less of him.

He could be honest with her about his other shortcomings. Amanda had accused him of being closed off, and he couldn't deny it. He tended to doubt the sincerity and motivations of anyone who expressed a romantic interest in him, and that was hardly a recipe for a trusting relationship. It was part of him—he'd tried to fix it, but couldn't. It was how he was made.

Gracie emerged from the bathroom at last, a

single lamp on her side of the bed illuminating the hotel room.

'Do you want me to put some pillows between us?' he asked.

She looked at him blankly.

'I mean, so we don't accidentally bump each other. For privacy?'

'Oh, yes, good idea.'

She turned and went to the small cupboard, but after she looked inside, she turned back, frowning. 'There aren't any spares. I could call the concierge?'

'If you want,' he replied.

She paused at the open closet for a moment.

'That seems like overkill,' she said.

'Yes. Besides, we're exhausted. I'm sure we'll both be asleep quickly.'

She nodded.

He lay on his back as Gracie exposed the sheets on her side of the bed. She was wearing a T-shirt that came to the middle of her thighs. She climbed in but stayed right on the edge of her side of the bed.

'You can move closer. I don't bite. You don't want to roll out. If one of us is going to end up on the floor, we should start like that.'

He noticed a shy smile on her face as she inched slightly closer to him and then turned out the light.

The room fell into darkness. His eyes searched for some sort of light, but he could see very little, not even shadows or large shapes. The town they were in was so small, no ambient light came in from behind the edge of the curtain.

He wore a T-shirt and underpants. He ran warm, and in the late summer, if he'd been alone in his own bed, he wouldn't have worn anything.

In the darkness, he was even more aware of his body than he'd been before. Muscles he was unaccustomed to using. Despite reapplying sunscreen throughout the day—Gracie was as careful about sunscreen as she was about water safety—his skin was still tight. He felt the beginnings of a cramp in one of his legs and reached down to massage it. The cramp subsided, but his shoulder began to ache, and he had to roll over to get comfortable.

In the process, his arm brushed against hers.

'Sorry,' he said.

'We both need to stop apologising,' she said. To emphasise the point, she touched his arm. They both stilled. Skin touching skin, warmth on warmth and the memory of her wet body in his arms that afternoon travelled straight from his brain to his belly. She moved her soft arm against his, and her fingers slipped through his like puzzle pieces slotting together. He tightened his fingers around hers, and the rest of his body and brain went into overdrive.

Usually if he was attracted to someone, it was relatively straightforward—he'd ask if they felt it as well. Explain that he was only looking for something casual, ensure he wore protection, ensure they understood he wasn't in it for the long term.

Women often thought they wanted a serious thing with him—but they didn't know him. They were attracted to the *idea* of him. A person who didn't exist. Not the real him.

Gracie was different because she knew him. He couldn't give her his prepared speech about only being interested in a casual relationship. They were already friends. They already had more than a physical connection. They had a professional one as well.

Besides, Gracie was different. She lived in the real world where, he suspected, slightly different rules and expectations applied than in the ambitious and heated world of show business.

She rolled onto her side. The only parts of their bodies that touched were their hands, his thumb drawing circles in her palm, her fingers sliding in and out between his, every movement sending a new spark into his chest.

If he found holding her hand this erotic, he wasn't sure he could withstand anything more.

'Gracie, I went looking for the swim instructor code of conduct,' he said through a rough throat.

She snatched her hand away from his, and he felt her body tense through the mattress.

'What are you talking about?'

'I checked if there are any rules about swim instructors and their pupils.'

She exhaled, and he felt her breath in his chest.

'I don't think there are any rules about consenting adults, but of course it's all irrelevant if you don't feel the same way,' he said.

There. He'd laid it all out. Risked their whole relationship in the process, but his body couldn't let it go. The memory of her legs around his waist, her lips on his, her sigh in his throat. Her fingers looped through his just moments ago. Rubbing back and forth, the way her smooth skin felt against every goosebump on his.

Beside him he heard a sigh, part anguish, part surrender.

And then small fingers slid down his arm and back into his hand. He traced a circle in her palm with his thumb. Once. Twice.

'I'm only here for a while. I think whatever this is between us has a natural end date, if that's what you're worried about,' he said.

'It's one of the things I'm worried about.'

'What else are you worried about?' he asked.

'The media, your fame. Though I guess I'm already caught up in that.'

'Are you worried about anything in this room right now?'

'No.'

'Nor am I. The two people in this room are the ones I'm most certain of.'

'I feel the same way,' she whispered.

Gracie knew all about him, and she still liked

him. He longed to hold her in his arms when water and lessons were not involved. To just be with her. To wrap himself up in her.

He rolled towards her, onto his side. They faced one another, her breathing rapid, his pulse just as quick. In the dark they could only feel their way to one another. They reached for each other at the same time, warm skin against warm skin. Her soft lips against his hungry ones.

His body remembered hers from their previous kiss, her taste already familiar, her smell like coming home. The way her neck smelt of the orange in her soap, the way her hair still smelt of the sea. He knew her. He knew the sound of her sighs, the way the side of her neck was sensitive. From all the hours in the pool, he knew the strength she carried in her small frame. The way their bodies fit improbably yet perfectly together.

The darkness heightened everything, the silkiness of her skin, the sharpness of her nipples through the thin fabric of her T-shirt.

'Do you mind if we turn a light on?' she asked.

'Mind? Are you kidding?' He couldn't wait to see her.

'I want to see you. It seems pointless to make love to the great Connor Day if I can't see him.'

His body turned to lead.

'Wait, Gracie, I'm still me. Connor who can't swim. I need to know it's me you're with. Not some fictional character.'

She stiffened, then drew away.

Damn.

He'd messed it up again. Without even realising what he was doing. But he wanted Gracie to want him, not some fantasy of him. The soft light beside her side of the bed came on, and he blinked.

Gracie was sitting, and he pulled himself up as well. Discombobulated. Confused. He'd thought things were going so well. Turned out he was wrong again.

She took his face in her hands, traced lines down his cheek, down his chest, examined him. 'You know what, I don't think you're as perfect as they say. Like right here, there's a freckle. How did this get here? How did anyone allow it?'

'Ha-ha.'

'Connor, just so you know, I don't much like any of the characters you've played. And the famous movie star? He did nothing for me. The person I'm here with now is the one I like the most. Every single version of Connor is gorgeous, and that's just a fact. But it's you I want to see. You I want to make love with. Not the others.'

Connor lay on his back and closed his eyes to steady himself.

Gracie didn't lie. He doubted she was capable of it. He wanted to believe every word she said. He trusted her to catch him. He trusted her to save him.

He opened his eyes. He sat up and reached for

her, lifting her easily onto his lap. She straddled him, their faces level, reminding him so much of their position in the surf, her legs wrapped around his. Their bodies holding and supporting one another. His height, her strength.

Connor lifted his hand to her shoulders, slid it up her neck and into her luxurious hair. Her eyes closed, her mouth hung open, and when she exhaled, he imagined all of her own worries were slipping away. She leant into him, and their lips reunited. He loved the taste of her, the softness of her lips and the sweetness of her mouth. All of it. She tugged at his bottom lip, teased his tongue with hers. Then drawing away to look at him. Her eyes open and bright. As excited as he felt. She was pushing him to the edge and then pulling him back again. But just as he did in the water with her, he felt safe. The gentle push and pull, the irresistible drag and dip as she kissed him and rubbed herself against his hard length. Then the deepening, the quickening when he lay on top of her and it was his turn to undress her and taste his way over and down her curves.

'I want this. Do you have protection?' she asked just when he thought he couldn't wait any longer. He retrieved a package from his bag, and his fingers trembled as she helped sheath him. She slid down him, her lips branding their way as she went, on his neck, across his nipples, over his heart. By the time she took him inside her with a moan, he was already on the edge of losing control.

He memorised it all. Every gorgeous square inch of her perfect body. The way her lids hung heavy and low when he hit just the right part of her. The way her face broke when she came apart. But then he buried his face in her shoulder. She couldn't see his face. She couldn't see what she was doing to his insides, to his heart and to his soul. He wasn't ready for that.

# CHAPTER EIGHT

'How are you feeling?'

Gracie groaned, brought her mind back into her body.

'Stiff, sore.'

'In a good way?'

She smiled to herself. 'Definitely.'

The skin on her neck and shoulders was tight from the extra sun she'd had yesterday. Her thighs and arms were sore from all the swimming. And the rest of her? Also feeling unaccustomed to the workout she'd had last night. But none of it was bad. It was, she decided, a very good feeling indeed.

'Feel like getting back in the water?' she asked.

'I do. But first I'd like a big breakfast and an even bigger cup of coffee.' He smiled down at her, and her skin prickled. From somewhere inside her, excitement bloomed and expanded in her limbs, in her chest, in her belly.

Connor leant towards her, and she reached for him. The thrill of just being able to do that was not getting old. The ability to touch Connor Day whenever she wanted to, and even better, to have him lean in towards her in return, was addictive.

His lips met hers, not for show this time, but because they both wanted to. His lips trailed a path down her neck to her collarbone. She shivered.

She wanted to ask him what he was thinking, but he'd been clear last night when he'd said that whatever was between them had a natural end date.

It was only the security and certainty of this that gave her the courage to do what they'd done last night. The freedom to let herself go this morning. This might not be their pretend relationship, but it also wasn't her real life. In much the same way she was pretending to be Connor's girlfriend, now she was pretending to be the type of person who could be his lover. Confident, relaxed, sure of herself.

It was sensible.

'How are you feeling?' she asked as he kissed behind her ear.

'Also sore. But in a good way. A very good way.'

A natural end date. For as long as he was in the country. Or as long as the fake relationship had to last. She was already pretending to be someone she wasn't. She could go the extra mile for a few weeks.

'Method acting?' she teased.

He laughed. 'What are you talking about?'

'I'm really getting into the role of your girlfriend. Really living it.'

He laughed again.

'If you like,' he said, taking one of her breasts into his mouth and making her sigh again.

They ordered an enormous breakfast into their room and ate on the balcony that overlooked a park and the water. Eggs, bacon, pancakes, fresh fruit, sourdough toast and jam. A giant pelican glided over the water, and like the bird, she tried to suspend herself in the moment. Beautiful. Weightless. Impossible.

They checked out and drove back to the waves at Cave Beach. She was pleased, and not a little proud, to see how strong and confident he was becoming in the surf. She could hardly believe that just less than two weeks ago, he couldn't swim a stroke.

Now there were times, particularly when they embraced one another in the water, delighting in the way their bodies felt floating together, that they weren't student and teacher, or even Connor Day and Gracie Sutherland, but two other people entirely.

He was becoming very competent and confident in the waves, though it still bothered her that she didn't understand exactly what was going to be required of him in his role. Where exactly he would have to swim, how long the scene was, what the director required of him. Virginia had assured her that her job wasn't to attend the set or ensure it was all safe or anything like that, but still she would have felt better—and felt better for Connor—if she knew what he was going to have to do.

Yet he had been reluctant to talk to her about the movie ever since the day she'd first told him about Caroline. She didn't blame him, but at some point, they'd have to discuss what he needed to do in the ocean. In *the* scene.

But not now.

Not when everything was so perfect.

They were back in Sydney before she knew it, and certainly before she had time to wrap her head around the change in their relationship. She couldn't even tell anyone she was with Connor Day, because everyone already thought they were a couple.

Everyone except Virginia.

She'd had several messages from Virginia (compelling her to call her with an update), but Gracie just slipped her phone away.

It wasn't that she thought Virginia wouldn't approve—on the contrary—but her friend wouldn't understand the arrangement she and Connor had. Virginia would tell her not to hold back emotionally. Not to dismiss the whole idea of a relationship when it had barely begun.

And Gracie couldn't explain it to her. She didn't want anything to intrude on this pretend, fragile world that would be her life for just a few more weeks.

In public, Connor Day's girlfriend. Behind closed doors, his lover. Pretending everywhere.

Gracie woke early. It was Connor's first day on set, and he'd likely be gone most of the day. He was showering, and she'd decided to take control of the coffee machine first before he could mess it up. She made two strong cups and waited for him to finish his shower.

One of the many copies of the script that seemed to follow Connor wherever he went lay on the bench. This was the one covered in notes, highlighter strokes and more than a few coffee mug rings.

Gracie looked at it. She wanted to pick it up. She wanted to know what the movie was about. She figured she needed to know what the scenes in the water involved. She wanted to make sure he was confident in those.

'Gracie.'

The sound of his voice usually made her insides melt, but this time she jumped.

'You can read it if you like, but you don't have to.'

'I know.' She passed him his coffee. 'Maybe you could just tell me what you need to do in the water. I want to help you practice the scene.'

'What do you want to know?'

'For instance, will it be filmed in the real ocean? Will there be a stunt person?'

Connor stepped up to the bench and pulled out one of the stools for her. Then he took one for himself.

'The real ocean. Mostly. There will be a stunt person, but as you know, I need to be able to swim for my own safety.'

'Yes. And for the safety of anyone around you. But I also want you to feel comfortable shooting this scene. Should I come to the set?'

He shook his head. 'The stunt team can help me with it.'

'Yes, but…'

'The thing is, Gracie, it's a distressing scene. A child is going to drown. I'm going to be struggling in the water.'

'Yes, but not really. Neither of those things will happen in real life. You might look like you're struggling, but you won't be really.'

'I don't want to ask more of you than we already have.'

Oh.

'Are you just saying this to protect me? Because I'll be fine.'

She wanted to be imposed on, didn't she? She wanted to help. This role was becoming as important to her as it so obviously was to him.

'What happens in the movie?'

'Gracie, we don't have to talk about it.'

'I know. I don't want to know everything. I just

want to know how it ends. Is it a happy or a sad ending?'

'Can it be both?'

'Sad ending with a ray of hope?'

'Something like that.'

'What happens to him, your character? The one who blames himself.'

Connor shook his head. 'I don't think that's important.'

'Maybe not, but I'd like to know how they cope.'

'Their marriage ends. His wife moves on. There's no indication that he does.'

'Right,' she said, though there was nothing right about it. She wasn't even sure why she needed to know, or why it was at all important whether a fictional man in a totally different situation to hers was happy or not.

Connor picked up her hand. 'It's just a movie. It's not a blueprint or an advice manual. You can make up your own story.'

She shook her head. 'I'm not looking for any advice. I'm just fine.'

'Yes, you get by. But don't you want to soar? Don't you want your life to be as amazing as it could be?'

Gracie looked down. No. Fine was safe. And safety was everything. Making life amazing also meant risking total and utter destruction if fine was taken away.

'No. I like things as they are,' she said simply.

Teaching lessons, tending her garden, playing with Biscuit. Swimming in the ocean with Connor. Making love with Connor.

Being with someone she trusted more and more each day. Being with someone who, like he said, made her heart soar.

He finished his coffee and pulled her into a hug.

'I have to go. I hope you have a good day.'

She nodded. She had no plans. Just the empty space he'd left behind.

Gracie was bored out of her mind within an hour of Connor leaving.

Usually she was happy with her own company, able to occupy herself.

*But that's when you have a full-time job and no housekeeper and can come and go as you please.* This wasn't like that at all. Leanne was doing everything for her, and after opening the front gate and spying the cars waiting in the street with their camera lenses, she decided she didn't feel like a walk after all.

She scrolled on her phone until she saw a post with a photo of her and Connor in the surf at Hyams Beach. It had been taken two days ago. The headline was friendly, though, reporting how much in love they seemed.

She grinned. The photo had been taken before they had shared a bed.

She kept scrolling. The very next thing was a

photo of Connor leaving his house—the house she was currently sitting in—that very morning, with a caption speculating that their relationship was over based on nothing except the fact that Connor was alone.

Gracie laughed.

Wow. Just wow.

She knew she shouldn't believe everything she read in the media, but the way in which the two posts were so wrong would have been terrifying if it weren't so funny.

Moments later, Virginia called. Her office at White Horses was behind her on the screen. Gracie was sitting outside by the pool, with the view of the harbour behind her on the screen.

'Nice view. So you're back from your South Coast adventure?'

'Yes, and according to the internet, we are both happily in love and broken up.'

'You know you can't believe everything you read. Which one is it?'

'The truth?'

Virginia nodded.

'Well, I'm pregnant with twins, and he's hooking up with a co-star. The media have it all wrong.'

'Way to avoid my less-than-subtle question. You and Connor? How's it going?'

'Fine. Good. He's really doing well. He's becoming a strong swimmer.'

'Great. And the two of you? How are you getting along?'

She hesitated, not because she didn't trust her friend but because the lines between reality and make-believe felt too porous. If she said the words out loud, *I'm sleeping with Connor*, it might become something it wasn't.

'We are getting along well. He's a really lovely guy. Very…normal.'

'He doesn't have two heads.'

'You know what I mean. He's not stuck up at all, really easy to be around.'

Virginia smiled. 'It's okay. You don't have to tell me.'

'There's nothing to tell!'

'Of course not. Is he there? Can he hear this conversation?'

Gracie shook her head. 'No, he's on set. I'm here by myself.'

'Lovely.'

'I thought it would be, but to be honest, I don't know what to do with myself.'

'It won't be forever,' Virginia said. 'Just a few weeks.'

Several days ago, that thought would have given her comfort. Now she wanted the relationship to last almost as much as she wanted it to end.

'There is something I've been thinking about. Our swimming support fund,' Gracie said.

It was a fund that White Horses kept to fund

lessons for children who couldn't afford them. So many times, they'd seen children start lessons and then families withdraw if they went through difficult financial times. Sometimes funding the lessons for a month or two kept the kids in classes over the long term.

'What about it?'

'We've always talked about raising money for it, but I haven't known where to begin, and you don't have the time. I have lots of time now,' she pointed out.

'But how? What would you do?'

'I suddenly have a social media following. I know famous people. Well, one famous person. There must be something I could do to raise money for it. I don't know. How do people raise money for this sort of thing?'

'I don't know, either. I'm guessing you're thinking more than the sausage sizzle we hold once a year?'

'Yes, but what?'

'Gracie, darling, I have to go. But it's a great idea. You should look into it.'

Virginia ended the call.

Gracie didn't know where to start, but she reasoned that she had all day to find out. She began by looking up charities she did know about. There were charities in the US that arranged lessons for free for children who couldn't afford it.

How did they raise money? How did they manage the money?

She didn't have the first idea how to raise money for charity, but she now had time to learn.

Connor left the studio as soon as he'd finished his scenes. Often he would stay to support fellow cast members, but he was conscious Gracie had been by herself all day.

It was good to be coming home to someone and not an empty house or hotel room. Someone he could talk to about his day. He enjoyed the camaraderie that built up on some productions, but working and socialising so close together could become slightly claustrophobic. Stepping away each evening and going home to Gracie was a relief and got his head out of the role. He'd love to always be able to do that.

Of course, that would have to be with someone who wasn't Gracie. She wasn't going to upend her life for his *circus*, and he'd never ask her to. Besides, she'd broken off her last engagement rather than leave her parents.

He just had to enjoy this while it lasted.

When his driver dropped him back at the house, he spied several cars with photographers inside them. Gracie would be safe inside, but if she had left the house at all today, she would have encountered them.

She was on the couch engrossed in something

on her laptop when he came in. She looked up and beamed. 'How was it?'

She looked so excited, so hopeful, and somehow it put everything that had happened in his day into perspective.

'Good, really good.' Sure, there were ups and downs and minor annoyances, but he was proud of what he'd done, what they'd all achieved, and it felt good to say it.

'Great. Are you exhausted, or do you want to have a swim?' she asked.

'I am tired, but I think a swim might help. Is that weird?'

'Not all. Let's do it.'

She closed her laptop and stood.

His body instantly felt better when he got into the water. It surrounded and supported his tense muscles, and he felt relaxed and invigorated at the same time. Practicing his strokes increased his confidence and stretched his tired muscles. Gracie watched him and gave occasional pointers, but didn't need to say much. He was getting there. He could, he sometimes allowed himself to think, actually swim. It was a strange concept to get his head around, much less say. After all the years of lying and pretending, now he didn't have to anymore.

It wasn't a huge thing. It wasn't as though his inability to swim had haunted him every day, but it had been something lurking quietly in the back of his psyche, reminding him he wasn't good enough. Reminding him that there were things he'd always need to hide about himself. Because his father mustn't ever find out the truth. Because he had to keep them all safe.

And now it was all okay! Now he could swim. He'd somehow managed to fix the past, to right wrongs. Soon no one would ever know the real truth about him or his family. The biography in his Wikipedia entry, the story the world believed about his happy, stable childhood, would actually be true.

Shedding these worries and their weight made him feel more buoyant than he could ever remember feeling. As weightless as he had felt jumping the waves with Gracie.

Out on the deck by the pool, in their wet swimmers, they ate the dinner Leanne had made for them. The light began to fade. Still wrapped in their towels, they moved together to the outdoor sofa that overlooked the harbour and watched the colours of the sky and water change.

He pulled her close to him, under his arm, against his chest. She tucked her knees up under her.

'Did you get up to much today?' he asked.

'I didn't go out, if that's what you mean.'

She guarded her privacy and peace fiercely and knew she was happy to be out of view of the photographers. Yet he caught the edge of sadness in her voice.

'Are you going a little stir-crazy?'

'Maybe a little.'

'Well, I might have a solution. An outing.'

'Okay.' She sat up straight.

'I've been invited to lunch this Sunday. I should say, *we've* been invited to lunch this Sunday.'

He deliberately did not to add, 'Because we need to pretend you are my girlfriend.' Even though he was increasingly forgetting that they were putting on a show for the cameras. That Gracie had agreed to pretend to be his girlfriend when they also had another, more private, arrangement.

'Sure. Who with?'

'With some people from work. As guests of Thibault Martin.'

She looked at him blankly, then shrugged.

'He's the owner of Grand Ecran Productions.'

This also didn't spark any recognition, and he realised what a bubble he lived in as part of the show business world.

'It's a film production company, the one making my movie.'

Finally recognition dawned. 'Oh, so your boss.'

'If you like.'

'And a big deal?'

He nodded. Grand Ecran was one of the largest production and distribution companies in Europe.

Martin was very influential. Not only in Europe but throughout the world.

'So we have to be on our best behaviour.'

He grinned and pulled her closer. 'I can't imagine you being anything but.'

'I mean, we have to stick to our story. About us. How we met. How I'm not teaching you.'

About the fake relationship? The fake relationship that was now real, but temporary? That story? He felt her embrace slacken. She pulled away, sensing what he knew. The lie about him being able to swim kept rising up between them. But they had to keep his secret.

'Yes, no one can know you're teaching me to swim, but hopefully the part about us being together will be easier to lie about now.'

She narrowed her eyes, considering his description of their relationship. They weren't in a serious relationship or in love, as they were pretending to be, but they were more than friends. He didn't want to lead her on, have her believe otherwise. But he also didn't want to raise expectations he couldn't deliver on.

*'It has a natural end date.'*

To his relief, she nodded and moved back closer to him, tucking herself under his arm and against his chest again.

'I have a favour to ask you as well,' she said.

'Anything,' he replied.

She moved away from him and faced him, eyes

sparkling, her whole face aglow. With her feet still tucked underneath herself, she was practically bouncing.

'Virginia and I run a small fund. We run one event a year, usually a low-key local thing, a sausage sizzle.'

'Sausage sizzle?'

'A sausage on a piece of bread with sauce and onion. Favourite Australian way of raising money for charities. It's practically your patriotic duty to buy one when you come across a stand.'

'Are you serious?'

'Mostly. Anyway, that's not the point. The point is, sausage sizzles are small-time. I was scrolling through social media this morning.'

'Gracie!' What speculation had she seen about herself? Connor and most people he knew gave social media a wide berth. He had people to check things for him, tell him what to post and when, so he didn't have to look too closely at all.

'It's okay. I get it. I knew even at the time that I should leave it alone. Did you know we're having twins *and* breaking up?' She laughed.

'I'm glad you can still laugh about it.'

'I can. And you see, I started to think how bonkers it is that I suddenly have so many followers. Yes, yes, nowhere near as many as you, but you know what I mean. The other mad thing is that White Horses now has thousands more as well.

So I was talking to Virginia and thinking about our fund.'

'And?'

'And I thought it would be a shame to waste my fifteen minutes. That we could do better than a sausage sizzle.'

'To raise money?' She was so excited about her idea, he wasn't sure he was following.

'Exactly!'

'And? What was the favour?'

'Nothing outrageous. Something you're comfortable with. Do you have any ideas for ways to promote the fund? Something you could donate, maybe. I've been reading up about it and how celebrities donate their time or something they own.'

That was easy. He'd done this sort of thing a few times before over the years. Auctioned off a dinner with a fan. Raffled tickets to film premieres.

'Of course, Gracie, anything.'

'Great! Even if we just auctioned off the chance to meet you, we could raise enough to put several kids through.'

'Through what?'

'Swimming lessons. That's what the fund is for.'

'Oh.' Pennies dropped slower than they should have. 'Your fund, it's about swimming lessons?'

'Yes, for kids who don't have the money.' He saw the moment she sensed his reservations, and her face fell. 'I figured this would be something you'd love to do. Since you never had the opportunity to learn.'

His chest felt leaden, but he forced a smile. 'I am. It's a great idea.'

'But it's a secret. You not knowing how to swim.' She scrunched up her face.

'I have to keep it a secret. It's very important.' *More, even, than you realise.*

'Because of your contract.'

He nodded. It wasn't a total lie. A white lie. It was in his contract. That they would keep the secret. It was just that it had been his request, not the studio's.

'It's complicated.' It was. There were so many reasons he didn't want the world to know it had taken him until he was in his thirties to learn to swim. It might seem a minor thing to some people, but it wasn't about vanity. It was about sticking to the story he'd always told about his family. It was about protecting the people he loved.

'Why?'

'Because… I'd have to clear it with the producers and the marketers and everything like that. A lot of time and money goes into how a movie is promoted, what tone we need to take, the whole package. I can ask them. But I don't want you to get your hopes up.'

She sat back, well and truly deflated.

'I'll ask, I promise.' And he meant it. It probably wasn't a big deal. 'It'll be fine. I'm just being paranoid. They might love the idea.'

'It's getting late. We should call it a day.' She stood, pulling her towel tight around herself.

'Gracie, is it such a big deal to you, me lying about knowing how to swim?' he asked, uneasy.

'What do you mean?'

'Is there any way you'd agree with their decision to keep it a secret?'

'I just don't get it. It's nothing to be ashamed of. If any of the adults there that day Caroline drowned had known, then someone might have been able to save her. If I'd been a better swimmer… I just don't understand the need for secrecy.'

'It's about the movie. I don't think it's the direction they want to go to promote it.'

'I'm far from an expert, but don't the people who vote for the Academy Awards love that sort of thing? Drastically changing your appearance? Doing an amazing accent? Achieving some sort of physical feat?'

He shrugged, even though she had made a good point. It was something Bruce had also pointed out when Connor had first been offered the role. 'It takes more than a different accent or putting on weight to win an award. And…honestly, I'd like everyone to think I've given a good performance regardless of my swimming ability. I don't want people to praise my acting just because I learnt a new skill.'

She frowned.

He'd been feeling so light, so hopeful. And now? Now he was on tenterhooks again. Out of seemingly nowhere, they'd had an argument.

He sighed and went to her. 'I'm sorry, I really am. It's complicated. But I will help you with the fund in any way I can. You're right. It's an excellent cause.'

She hugged him tight, her hair damp and skin warm against his own. Some of his worries dissolved. It would be okay. He would tell her one day. When the time was right.

# CHAPTER NINE

A LARGE SHADOW moved over them. Gracie tipped her head back, looking up at the grey underside of the magnificent bridge as the yacht sailed under it. Even as a Sydneysider, she never became immune to the spectacular sight of the enormous bridge, the white sails of the Opera House and the tall buildings of the city surrounding it all. Though she'd never seen it quite from this angle before.

They had sailed around many of the gorgeous coves tucked around the foreshore and now cleared the bridge towards Darling Harbour and Balmain. Each turn revealed a different sight.

She was wearing the linen dress she'd bought in the boutique on the coast. Luckily it seemed to be just the thing, as the other women were dressed in much the same way. It was a small party, less than a dozen people, most of whom she'd met at the cast and crew party.

Their hosts were Thibault Martin, the French owner of the studio producing Connor's film, and his wife, Elise.

Giselle and her wife, Jenny, were also on board,

as well as Connor's manager, Bruce, who she had heard so much about. The man who'd convinced Connor his swimming lessons should remain a secret. Gracie gravitated to Giselle and her wife, feeling that she probably had more in common with Jenny than any of the glamorous people on the yacht. But Gracie still didn't take her eyes far from Connor. She felt better knowing that he wasn't far away.

'You make such a great couple,' Giselle said, noticing the frequent looks she and Connor were sharing. 'Everyone thinks so.'

'We do?' Gracie knew Connor was a good actor, but her ability to convince the world she was something she was not surprised her.

'He's so smitten. He leaves the set each day as soon as his scenes are over.'

'So?' Her pulse fluttered in her throat. Why would that be unusual?

'Usually we'd hang out. Practice lines if necessary, that sort of thing. Go for a drink.'

Giselle was just being polite. Making small talk. It was the kind of thing people said, wasn't it?

Gracie smiled, unsure how to respond, when she was becoming less and less sure about what was real and what wasn't.

It wasn't just Giselle. The other women on the yacht were also keen to remark on Gracie and Connor's relationship.

'I can see by the way he can't take his eyes off you that he's head over heels,' Elise Martin said.

She was a beautiful woman, about the same age as Gracie's mother. Unlike her parents, the Martins were full of confidence and joie de vivre. Elise was regaling them all with stories of their last holiday with two famous Hollywood actors, who they were good friends with. Elise was talking about this couple as Gracie might talk about Virginia and her husband. Fondly, casually, as though they weren't incredibly wealthy and successful.

She patted Gracie's hand and said, 'But I understand that it must be difficult for you. The attention, the newness of it all.' Elise's eyes were full of empathy. And a hint of sadness, which made Gracie nod.

'Believe it or not, I don't go lunching on yachts every day of the week,' Gracie said.

Elise laughed. 'Nor do I.'

'This is actually my first time on Sydney Harbour in anything but a ferry.'

Elise leaned close and whispered, 'Mine too. Oh, don't get me wrong, I'm amazingly fortunate, and Thibault and I have a wonderful life. We get to travel to so many places, meet so many amazing people, present company included, but he works very hard. Too hard. Trips like this are few and far between.'

Elise looked over at her husband almost wistfully, then turned back to Gracie. 'But this isn't an about me. We're celebrating.' She reached for the champagne bottle and topped up their glasses.

'We are?'

'To new friends, and new beginnings.'

Gracie sipped her wine and couldn't help feeling sad that she had been a good enough actress to trick everyone into believing her relationship with Connor was just beginning when, by Gracie's calculations, their relationship was already half over.

'What are we drinking to?' Jenny asked, sitting next to Gracie. Elise topped up her glass, too.

'To new beginnings. And of course love. Because without love, none of this matters,' Elise said.

Gracie glanced around the yacht. At the spread of seafood lunch and decadent desserts lying before them. At the champagne in its icy bucket.

Love was important, Gracie knew, but just how much hit her afresh with the suspicion that not everyone on this yacht, as privileged as they all were, was as happy as they appeared to be.

'My sons are about your age,' Elise continued. And it was on this point that Gracie finally thought she understood the source of the Frenchwoman's sadness.

'And what do they do?'

'Ah, various things.'

There was definitely a story there, but Elise didn't get a chance to elaborate as Connor joined them. Jenny moved along the bench to make room for him, but Connor sat flush against Gracie anyway, their thighs pressed against one another's, his hand on her knee. She felt instantly more relaxed when Connor was within reach. If they weren't on a billionaire's luxury yacht, on Sydney Harbour with a bunch of movie stars, she might have felt almost normal. Almost.

'Now, tell me, do you have an outfit for the premiere?' Elise asked.

Gracie shook her head. 'I'm not going to a premiere.'

'Oh, yes, you have to come. It's for *Sanctuary*. A new film from the studio. That's why we've come all the way to your side of the world.'

It hadn't even occurred to Gracie that the Martins' trip might be for something other than a holiday.

'We're sailing up the coast for a while, but we will be back in Sydney in a few weeks. Please come. Both of you,' she implored. 'Thibault, darling!' Elise called across the boat. 'You must ask Connor and Gracie to the premiere of *Sanctuary*.'

Thibault beamed and walked over to their side of the yacht. He placed his hand on Connor's shoulder. 'Of course you both must come.'

Jenny leant over and explained to Gracie, 'Giselle starred in this film last year, and it's being launched in Sydney since Giselle and Gerry are both here at the moment. Shooting one movie and promoting another at the same time isn't ideal, but it happens.'

'Are you going?' Gracie asked Jenny.

'Of course, I timed my visit for it. If you don't have anything to wear, come with me. We'll go shopping together.'

'I'd really like that.' Gracie smiled at Jenny. Out of the corner of her eye, she saw Connor's eyes crinkle in a silent question. *Are you okay?* they asked.

She nodded. She was fine. She was great. She was having a wonderful afternoon. Elise, Jenny and Giselle were terrific company. The breeze off the water lifted her hair, and the silver bridge was coming back into view.

*Step outside your comfort zone*, she reminded herself. *You never know, you might even have fun.*

Connor was having a good afternoon, but he wouldn't have called it relaxing. Thibault Martin was a powerful player in this business, and although he was a good guy, despite the gourmet lunch on a yacht on Sydney Harbour, Connor remained in professional mode. Plus there was the added stress of making sure Gracie was enjoying herself. Not to mention the fact that Bruce had surprised them all by arriving in Sydney.

He felt guilty that the level of fame he was subjecting her to was more than she'd signed up for. She was doing all of this to keep his secret, and putting her in situations like this made him even more aware of it. He had one eye and ear on her at all times. She seemed to be having a good time with the other women and had bonded with Jenny. Earlier, Elise had invited them both to the premiere of another Grand Ecran movie being held in Sydney in a few weeks.

It was unexpectedly nice, having someone at his side. Even if she wasn't literally beside him, he'd liked arriving with her, and he was already looking forward to going home together and talking about the day. It would be nice if she came to things like this with him in the future.

Which future? Next week, yes. Next month? Next year? No—probably not. Still, for a moment, he let his mind drift to the idea of Gracie being with him in LA. Or Boston. He'd love to show her the Common, the North End, his favourite bagel place. The real him. There was no point thinking about taking her to Boston—she'd never visit.

Bruce nudged him. 'You haven't said much about how the shoot is going. What do you think?'

'Good,' Connor said. 'I think.' He gave an equivocal shrug.

'I don't think his mind is completely on this movie, but on the pretty woman over there speaking to my wife,' Thibault teased.

Connor smiled, and Bruce laughed.

*Don't let on that it's a ruse.*

But Bruce didn't.

'She seems very lovely. What a coincidence, the way you met,' Bruce said.

Connor shot Bruce a sideways look that said, *Seriously?*

'Yes, it was—but these things do happen.'

'They do,' Thibault agreed. 'Elise and I met in an elevator.'

'An elevator?' Connor and Bruce said at once.

'Yes. Not a broken one or anything dramatic—just a ride fifty floors down in New York. We realised we were both French and started talking, and that…was that.'

Simple. So simple. Could love ever be that straightforward? Not in Connor's experience.

Jenny stood up and moved away, leaving the seat next to Gracie vacant. Before Connor could claim it, Bruce slid in.

Connor clenched a fist. He trusted Bruce but didn't like the idea of the two of them spending too much one-on-one time together.

He knew he had to tell Gracie the truth about why the lessons needed to remain secret—but not yet. The last thing he needed was Bruce accidentally saying something to alert anyone to the fact that his relationship with Gracie wasn't exactly what the world believed.

*You're always pretending. Everyone on this boat thinks you're in love. Only you and Gracie know the truth.*

And even that truth was becoming harder to pin

down. They were together, yet they were pretending. Like in the rest of his life, truth and reality were constantly being blurred.

Connor stopped listening to Thibault and tried to figure out what Gracie and Bruce were talking about, but they were speaking so closely their foreheads nearly touched.

'Excuse me,' he said to Thibault. 'I need to speak to Gracie.'

Thibault laughed and patted his back. 'Go, go! I can see you can't bear to be apart from her.'

Connor smiled. If only his reasons for going over were as pure as Thibault believed.

The others made room for him, and he took the vacant seat on Gracie's other side, sliding his hand around her shoulders. They smiled at each other, and he heard Elise ask, 'Gracie, will you be joining Connor in LA?'

He was still looking at Gracie and saw her take a very long blink—long enough that everyone would have noticed her hesitation.

'We… I…that is…' she stuttered.

'We have some logistics to sort out,' Connor said quickly, pulling Gracie closer. He was the actor, after all. 'But we're determined to make it work, aren't we?'

Gracie nodded and smiled weakly. 'Yes. We are.'

She didn't sound convinced, and his heart fell.

But why? Because she might expose their ruse—or because he wanted her to mean it?

*She's not going to LA*, he told himself. *And how could you expect her to?*

It wasn't even *his* favourite place in the world. The conversation shifted awkwardly to other matters, and as the wharf came into view, people began gathering their belongings and saying farewells.

Connor and Gracie stood on the bow side of the boat, and he pulled her close.

'Thank you for all of this,' he whispered into her hair.

'A luxury cruise isn't exactly a hardship.'

'But it wasn't entirely relaxing. I'm sorry Elise put you on the spot back there.'

'I'm sorry if I wasn't more effusive. I'm not an actress,' she said.

'Don't mention it. It would've been awkward even without our…circumstances.'

She nodded and turned her face away.

It would've been awkward even if their relationship were real and permanent. But in this strange limbo—lovers, yet not in love—it was agonising.

He noticed the life jackets and realised, for the first time, he'd know how to use one. An unexpected dip in the harbour would still be unpleasant—but he could tread water now. He could survive. That small, ordinary confidence felt miraculous.

And he had her to thank—not just for the swimming, but for keeping his secret.

'Thank you. For everything,' he said.

She turned back to him, her brow furrowing in question.

'This is the first time I've been able to relax on a boat. I didn't realise how stressful I found it until now. If I was pushed overboard, I'd know what to do. I could survive long enough for someone to throw one of those to me.' He nodded toward the lifesaver.

'Did you go on boats often?'

'Not often, but sometimes. I once had to shoot several scenes on a sailing boat in Greece and felt ill the whole time. I told everyone it was seasickness. They believed me.'

She squeezed his arm. 'I'm pleased for you that you did this. And not as your swimming instructor, but as your friend. I hope you feel better about a whole lot of things when you get home.'

It was so easy being with her. She knew who he really was, and she liked him anyway. He felt lighter than he had in years. Maybe ever.

Shortly afterwards, the Martins thanked everyone for a wonderful afternoon. With promises to see them at the premiere, the guests disembarked.

He slid his palm into Gracie's and entwined their fingers as they made their way to his waiting car.

'Excuse me.'

The voice behind them made him stop and Gracie's grip tighten. 'Connor Day? Are you Connor Day?'

The voice belonged to a young woman standing beside an even younger girl—a sister, perhaps.

'We're sorry to bother you, but could we please get a selfie? We think you're great. We're big fans.'

His heart fell for Gracie as she let go of his hand. This was part of his job, and he was well compensated for moments like this. Young fans were never any trouble. He could never say no to them.

'Of course.' He put on his best smile.

'Would you like me to take the photo?' Gracie offered.

Connor and the two girls looked at her, then at each other, silently conferring.

'That'd be great, thanks!' said the older one.

Gracie took the phone, and Connor posed with them—hands on his knees, bent to bring his face level with theirs. He smiled while she took a few shots.

'Thank you, Gracie,' said the youngest girl.

Gracie froze at the sound of strangers saying her name.

'We love you too! If I couldn't marry him, at least another girl from Sydney will!'

'Can we come to the wedding?' the younger asked.

'Oh no, I—' she began, but the girls giggled, the older one tugging the younger away before she could finish.

'Well done—your first celebrity encounter. How do you feel?'

'When I get over the shock that they knew my name and are apparently coming to our wedding, well… I guess it wasn't too bad.'

'The kids rarely are. I can't say no to them.'

'Of course not. And the adults?'

'Also usually no trouble.' At least not to him. He knew his female co-stars had a much harder time.

He was lucky.

And Gracie was lucky she'd soon be out of the public eye.

He took back her hand, which was now slightly clammy. He squeezed it once, wishing he could remind her their charade would all soon be over—and at the same time dreading that it would be.

They settled into as much of a routine as Connor's filming schedule would allow. Gracie filled her time researching fundraising and the rules around establishing a charity. She'd had a few conversations with Connor's publicity team about working together, but nothing had been firmed up yet.

She was feeling optimistic that raising money for White Horses would be something that she could do. As the days passed, most of the photographers seemed to give up, and some days none showed at all. Gracie had even snuck home on a few occasions to see her parents and Virginia, though she kept those visits brief. Her mother was full of questions Gracie couldn't answer. *When will we meet him? Is it serious?*

'Will you be moving to LA with him?' Sharon asked her again, point blank.

'No. Don't be ridiculous.'

'Why is it ridiculous?'

'I already told you that we agreed it'll only last as long as he's here.'

Her mother pulled a face and shook her head. 'I don't understand. You're absolutely glowing and clearly in love with him, yet you're telling me it isn't serious. What could possibly be holding you back?'

*Everything.*

'I'm a nobody swim instructor, and he's a world famous movie star. It's…complicated.'

Her mother harrumphed but didn't press further.

Gracie didn't fare much better with Virginia. It was somehow more difficult talking to her. Virginia knew that Gracie and Connor were meant to be pretending to be in a relationship and had a whole other set of questions.

'Are you in love with him?'

'No!' Her face was probably red. Not because she'd lied—she was definitely not in love with Connor Day—but because the question was so personal.

'Are you sleeping with him?'

This was where truth and lies began to blur. She was fake dating Connor, but not fake sleeping with him. They did have a physical relationship, but were only friends and definitely not the loved-up couple the world thought them to be.

Gracie answered Virginia's question by looking into her lap.

Virginia sucked in a loud breath. 'Gracie! That's wonderful.'

Gracie shook her head, and Virginia laughed.

'Are you saying he's bad in bed?'

'No!' she cried, which only made Virginia laugh harder.

'Tell me everything.' Virginia leant over her desk, but for the first time she could remember, Gracie couldn't talk to her friend about something. How could she explain to Virginia what was going on when she wasn't sure herself?

'It's nothing. It's just casual. We're friends. It's not like everyone is saying.'

Virginia smiled in a way that made Gracie break out in a cold sweat.

Going back to the swim school and her parents' place was awkward. She felt detached from her old life in a way that surprised—and unnerved—her.

The one place she did feel comfortable was with Connor, in his house, by his pool. That was the one place she felt like herself, where there was no need to lie to anyone. Connor knew who she was. She didn't have to think twice about what she did or said. They had no secrets.

And yet the one place that felt the most real was the one place that wasn't. Being with Connor wasn't her real life. It was an interlude. Almost like a holiday. In a short time, he would leave, and all her history with him would fade like a dream.

*You could go with him.*

Ha! They both knew that would never happen. To start with, they had an agreement. For as long as he was in Sydney. He had a whole other exciting life back in the States that she could never be a part of.

The next few weeks passed in a flash. One evening while Connor was showering after a swim, Gracie was absentmindedly flicking through the television channels. Her gaze kept flicking to the coffee table in front of her and the pile of scripts.

There were several copies floating around the house now. Some seemed to be newer versions, with fewer scribbles and stains, incorporating changes that had been made. Yet Connor still kept the previous versions, the ones with his notes in the margins. Like an old edition and a new edition of the same book. She glanced at the doorway, but he was still showering.

She picked up the script at the top of the pile. The page was folded to a particular scene.

Daisy: How can I help you if you won't talk to me?
Joel: I don't need your help.

Daisy: You need something more than a wine subscription service to help you deal with this.
Joel: I'm doing okay. Really.
Daisy: But maybe I'm not…

'What are you doing?'

She dropped the script at the sound of his voice.

'Snooping, sorry.' She straightened the pile of papers.

'You really don't have to read it,' he said.

'I know I don't.'

*But I'm looking for answers. I want to know how other people manage to set their guilt aside. Or how they manage to live comfortably with it.*

'I told you, it doesn't end happily.'

She sat on the sofa and he joined her, smelling of his orange-scented soap.

'What happens? After?' she asked.

They both knew that she meant after the child dies.

'My character can't deal with his guilt.'

'Understandable.'

'And his marriage unravels because he wants to forget it all ever happened.'

'But why should that matter?'

'Because his wife, Daisy, wants the kind of relationship where issues don't fester, where problems are spoken about and dealt with. Daisy wants that, but Joel can't give it to her.'

She blinked. Something about his comment felt

like a criticism, even though she knew he didn't mean it as one.

'Is it such a big deal? We all carry guilt, like we all carry our past. Everyone has baggage. Shouldn't she love him regardless? Maybe she needs to accept him, warts and all?'

He laughed. 'You should talk about this with Giselle. She has lots of views about Daisy. But I think the point is that he has to forgive himself. Daisy never blamed him for the death. She loved him for trying so hard to save the child. But she never blamed him. Joel thinks everyone around him blames him, but the only person who needs to forgive him is himself.' Connor looked at her, held her gaze and snagged her thoughts.

*He's talking about you.*

'It's understandable he can't forgive himself. Some things are unforgivable,' she said.

'Nothing is unforgivable if someone is truly sorry.'

'You don't really believe that, do you?'

He shrugged. 'I'm not talking about truly heinous crimes. But nor are we. We're talking about everyday people doing their best. Yes, I think most things are forgivable, especially when people are genuinely sorry.'

'When they atone for their mistakes?'

'Not even that. Gracie, you don't have anything to atone for.'

He *was* talking about her.

'I do. You don't understand.'

'You've spent your life trying to make it up to Caroline, to your parents. Your career, organising your life around your parents—and has any of it worked?'

'What do you mean?'

'None of it has cured your guilt, has it?'

'That's because I can never make it up to them.'

'Of course you can't, and you won't. But you have to forgive yourself. That's the only thing that will let you move on.'

'I have moved on.'

To Gracie's relief, he didn't call out her fib.

'Where's Biscuit? She hasn't greeted me this evening,' he said.

Nice way to change the topic.

The matter wasn't dealt with, but it didn't matter. They didn't have to deal with it. Better to enjoy their remaining time together without any added complications.

The following morning, they sat together on the couch. His laptop was open in front of them, and he was showing her photos of Boston as she'd wanted to see where he'd grown up. Connor didn't have to be at the studio until the afternoon, so they'd slept in, then gone for a swim. He entered the water without hesitation, performed the strokes automatically. He was a swimmer.

*I could even swim on my own.*

*'Never swim alone.'*

Well, that would happen eventually. Once he was home in LA. Alone.

Without Gracie.

At this point, the thing worrying him most about the film was his acting performance, and his conversation with Gracie the previous evening had intensified that worry.

He did believe—fervently—that she should forgive herself for her sister's death. That it hadn't been her fault. That carrying the guilt was preventing her from living and enjoying a full life.

Yet his character, Joel, couldn't forgive himself. Reconciling his personal views with the inconsistent ones of the character he was playing was difficult.

*It's called acting*, he reminded himself. *You want to be good at it, remember?*

Gracie snuggled into him, her head lazily resting on his shoulder. He breathed in the fresh scent of her hair.

'You smell good.'

'I smell like chlorine!'

'My new favourite smell.'

'Loser,' she teased.

He laughed because he most definitely was not. With Gracie against him, he felt like the luckiest man alive.

A window on the laptop screen popped open, and the computer sang with an incoming call. Gracie made to stand, but he pulled her back down. 'It's just my mom.'

'*Just* your mum?' she hissed.

'Please stay,' he said, answering the call right away so she had little choice.

'Connor, darling! I'm so glad I caught you!' said an attractive middle-aged woman with an accent just like Connor's. Though the similarities seemed to end there. Her hair and eyes were dark.

He rubbed his chin. 'Hi, yes, it's a tricky time difference. Mom, this is Gracie. Gracie, this is my mother, Sinead.'

Gracie smiled and waved. 'Hi, it's nice to meet you.'

'Oh, Gracie, you too. I'm glad he's got someone to keep him company all the way over there.'

'It's hardly the end of the earth,' Connor replied.

'It feels like that to me. What time is it there?'

'Eleven a.m.,' Gracie answered.

She was right to be hesitant about speaking to his mother. He hadn't briefed his family on the whole fake/not fake aspects of their relationship, but he wanted Gracie to meet his mother. And his mother to meet Gracie.

Another voice came from off camera. 'Is that Gracie? The girlfriend? Oh, can I meet her?'

'We can hear you, Yumi,' Connor said.

His sister-in-law's face appeared over his mother's shoulder. 'You were meant to. Gracie, hi, it's lovely to meet you. I'm Yumi.'

'Hi!' Gracie said again.

Yumi was quickly followed by his nieces, Hana and Naomi, and then his brother, Callum, until all five other members of his family were crowding around the camera to see Gracie. All talking at once.

'Hello!'

'Oh, she's pretty.'

'How's Sydney?'

'What do you do, Gracie? Are you an actress?'

'Are you bringing her to Boston?'

He picked up her hand and whispered, 'I'm sorry. I thought it would just be my mother.'

'Callum and Yumi and the girls are over for dinner, and I wondered if I'd catch you,' Sinead replied. 'Sorry about everyone, Gracie. How's the filming going, darling?'

'Good, I think—' was all Connor managed to say before Hana interrupted.

'Are you living together? He never lives with girls.'

'Shhh,' Callum said.

'Oh, I'm not living here, just staying while he's filming. It's easiest…' Gracie said.

'No need to explain. I wouldn't want to live with him either,' Callum said with a grin.

'Excuse me, I'll let you all catch up.' This time when Gracie moved to leave, he didn't stop her. She scooped up Biscuit and went to the back of the house.

'I'm glad you're with someone,' his mother repeated.

'Yeah, me too,' he said. There was no need to go into the ins and outs of their relationship. It was good. It might not be forever, but it was good for now.

'She's very pretty,' Naomi chimed in, and Connor had to agree.

'And she's really just someone you met by chance?' Yumi asked.

Connor nodded.

That's all they ever needed to know. His need to keep the lessons a secret was for his mother's sake. It was a good thing they would never meet Gracie in person.

'Yet another woman powerless in the face of your looks,' Callum joked. Callum took after their mother appearance-wise. 'Oh, how you suffer, big brother.'

'I think she likes me in spite of my appearance,' Connor admitted.

She did like him for him. He was certain. For the first time in such a long time, he was just Connor Day, regular kid from Boston and not a world famous star. He liked that. A lot.

He ended the call with a promise he never intended to keep, to bring Gracie to Boston, and went to find her. She was in the bedroom they were now sharing, stroking Biscuit.

'Hey, I'm sorry to put you on the spot like that. I thought it would just be Mom. I didn't reckon on all of them.'

He'd never thought of himself as having a large family, but from Gracie's perspective, his little clan would seem like a lot.

'It's okay. It was nice. Really. I just wasn't sure what you've told them. About us.'

He flopped onto the bed, stomach first. 'They only know the official line.'

She nodded. 'My parents too. Anything else seemed too complicated. I can't trust either of mine to keep the secret, and…well, it won't be for long.'

Her words hit harder than he expected. It was the truth, and he'd been careless enough to start forgetting and wondering otherwise.

'Your brother looks quite different to you,' she said.

'I take after my father.'

He felt queasy. He didn't mean to, but mention of his father often did that.

'Oh, right.'

He'd inherited his father's looks, his height. Possibly other things, too. His father was a classic charming man who had learnt at an early age that he could attract people with a smile. And then manipulate them with his words. To his great embarrassment, Connor found that he often could as well.

'Do you ever see your father?'

'Not if I can help it.'

'I'm sorry.'

'Don't be. I'm not.'

She lay down next to him, also on her stomach, and placed her arm over his back. He was tempted to roll over and pull her on top of him, but instead, he did something that felt far more intimate.

'Day isn't my real surname.'

It was Gracie's turn to be taken aback.

'I was born Connor O'Loughlin. When Mom left my father, she changed our name to Jones.'

'Her maiden name?'

'Definitely not. She wanted to make it difficult for him to find us. He wasn't…he wasn't nice. Not to us and especially not to her. We had to move a few times. We even lived in her car for a while.' His voice cracked, and it surprised him.

*It shouldn't. You never talk about this.*

Gracie reached for his hand and squeezed.

'I was reluctant to start modelling in case he happened to recognise me, but Mom assured me it would be okay. Time had passed, and the money was too much to refuse. She suggested I use the surname Day.'

'Why?'

'She said it sounded happy.'

'It does.'

'So, yeah, my first surname was O'Loughlin, and then it used to be Jones.'

She pressed her lips together and nodded.

'It's not unusual for stars to use different names, I think?'

'No. But I changed my name to protect my family, to make it more difficult for Dad to find us. Them.'

'Does he know who you are now? You're pretty…distinctive, and if you look like him…?'

'Yeah. He knows. He got in contact with me after my second movie.'

'And?'

'I spoke to him, asked him not to contact me. He hasn't since.'

'Are you worried about him? About what he might do?'

'No, not anymore. It was so long ago. Callum and I are both adults. We have the money and means to protect ourselves and our mother. But that doesn't mean I want a relationship with him. And it doesn't mean I want the world to know about our past. About his abuse of my mother. About everything we went through. I'm careful who I tell.'

'No, of course not. Thank you for telling me.'

'I've never really told anyone this, but I guess by now everything is out in the open between us. I feel like I could tell you anything.'

She smiled, and his heart pressed at his rib cage. Seeing her smile was worth more than any award or accolade. It was such a relief to tell her.

* * *

Gracie wasn't sure what she expected a film set to look like, but it wasn't this. This was a beach, one she'd visited before, but it had been closed to the public and all the roads around it blocked off. A singular feat for a popular Sydney beach. Tents and food vans made it look like some kind of festival, but there was no music, and the mood was tense. Almost sombre.

*It's just a movie. No one is actually going to die.*

Gracie clutched the lanyard they had given her to prove she was allowed to be there. She tried to stay out of the way but wanted Connor to notice her. They had gone round in circles about whether she should come. He didn't want her to be upset by the scene, but she wanted to make sure that if he needed guidance in the water, she would be there to help, and eventually he'd agreed. 'Besides, I've never been on a film set before. Let a girl see how the other half work.'

So he'd capitulated.

*'I think I could tell you anything.'*

Each time she recalled his words, she wanted to press her hands against her chest and hold the feeling there. Ever since he'd confided in her about his father, she'd felt even closer to him. They had both trusted one another with their deepest secrets. They'd built something special, and the feeling filled her with a sweet warmth.

Until she remembered it was temporary. Maybe

it was the fleeting nature of what they had that made it so precious. Either way, she was determined to savour their last week together. He only had a few more days of filming. Connor was returning to LA the day after the premiere of *Sanctuary*, Giselle's other movie.

The morning was bright, and she was glad they weren't going for some sort of cliché where disaster happened in a storm. Tragedies also happened on bright, cloudless days. Like this.

Connor spotted her, and a short while later, he strode over to her. He didn't look happy, yet once he was close enough, he wrapped her into an enormous hug. 'Thank you for coming,' he said into her hair. 'You're right, as usual. I feel better with you here.'

The unfamiliar products in his hair, the makeup on his face made him smell different, but she squeezed him back tightly.

'Tell me I can do this,' he whispered.

'Of course you can! Why are you asking me?'

'Because you believe in me.'

'Oh, Connor, I know you can. And not just the swimming. You've nailed that. But the rest of it as well. How long will it take?'

'It could be hours, until Gerry's happy we've got enough footage.'

'You do it more than once?' she whispered. She knew, in theory, that filming involved many takes, but experiencing it was a different thing.

'You don't have to stay all day.'

'I know, but… I want to be here for you.'

It didn't happen like a scene in a movie. There was so much stopping and starting. She was too far away to see everything, and as the day dragged on, the tension in her chest and throat began to ease. It wasn't realistic. The way they were structuring the scenes was almost clinical.

But then Connor dragged the boy out of the water and onto the sand.

She was relieved to see the boy was moving, but her heart hit her throat when she realised Connor was crying deep, guttural sobs. He tried to catch his breath at the same time he tried to give the boy CPR and yet, given his lack of breath, failed. The other actors moved around him, and a woman pushed him aside and began CPR.

*It's not going to work if you do it like that*, Gracie thought, and almost stood to go and show them the correct way. Thankfully she had the presence of mind to tell herself, *He's not really drowning*.

The child in the movie was safe and was not her sister.

Seeing Connor in this scene didn't remind her of the failed efforts to reach Caroline. She didn't even think of herself. She thought of her parents, her mother's cries, her father's struggle to lift his daughter out of the pool. Her parents, who had not arrived at the pool in time.

She thought of the other people who had been

there. The couple of hotel guests who had been sunbaking by the pool but who couldn't swim. Who had stood paralysed.

Did they blame themselves, too?

Probably, Gracie realised.

The paramedics who couldn't save her. It would have affected them as well.

Gracie had carried all the guilt herself, but many people and many factors had played a part in Caroline's death.

Could she forgive herself? Had she served a long enough penance?

*'I feel like I can tell you anything.'*

What did Connor mean by that? Did he mean he had feelings for her? Feelings that might even one day become like the feelings she had inside her chest when he smiled at her? Feelings of belonging? Of lightness?

The idea of saying goodbye to Connor was unthinkable.

Over the past few weeks, she'd become closer to him than anyone else in her life, shared things she'd never shared with anyone, and knew that he had shared things like that with her too. She trusted him, believed in him. The amazing, sexy movie star had been replaced by someone else— someone even more amazing. Someone even more wonderful. Her Connor.

The people near the cameras regrouped. The scenes was laid out again. Someone even rearranged the sand. The actors came out of character, got drinks, had their hair redone. Connor came over to her, wet, bedraggled.

He smiled shyly, and she squeezed his upper arm.

'It was amazing. You were amazing.'

He touched her arm too, like he wanted to hold her but didn't want her to get wet. He needed her, and she felt strangely part of this whole unfamiliar world.

'Connor! We need you,' a voice by the cameras called to him.

Gracie sat down to watch again. She lost count of the number of times they filmed, or attempted to film, the scene. Over and over she saw the rescue effort. All the people who were trying to save the boy, everyone was trying their absolute best. Over and over.

But the result was still the same.

So many events kept conspiring to prevent Connor from saving the child. It happened slightly differently in each take. Sometimes Connor got a grip on him, only to have his fingers slip. Other times waves stopped him reaching the child at all. Or he got a grip on the boy, and the director yelled *cut!* because Connor wasn't meant to save him. This happened enough times that the actor playing the child laughed and laughed. A badly timed wave was all it took to dislodge Connor's fingers from the boy's arm.

As the day dragged on, Gracie thought more and more about the day Caroline died. So many things had come together in the most horrible way. It wasn't just Gracie's fault for sneaking out. It wasn't the fault of the sunbathers who couldn't swim. It wasn't even her parents' fault, or the paramedics'. Or the fact the ambulance had been delayed by traffic. Maybe, just maybe, Gracie had to accept that what had happened hadn't come down to one particular factor or one particular person. Maybe she didn't have to carry the guilt alone.

Connor didn't think he'd ever been this exhausted. Gracie bundled him into the back of a car and directed the driver to Watsons Bay. She'd stayed on set all day, and he desperately hoped that was because she'd wanted to and not because she felt obliged. Connor was wrung out—physically and mentally. The scene had affected him. He'd hoped it hadn't upset Gracie.

But it was done.

The thing he'd been fearing for months, the thing he'd been devoting everything to, was done. He'd learnt to swim and then performed one of the most meaningful and emotionally difficult scenes he'd ever filmed.

And nailed it.

There'd even been a tear in Gerry's eye, and if a man who had directed several Oscar-winning performances had responded like that, Connor knew he'd done the best he could. Awards weren't the point. He'd produced a performance worthy of the greats, and that was enough for him. He was enough.

All he wanted was Gracie. And a bed and to sleep for twenty hours straight wrapped around her. He reached for her hand across the back seat and squeezed it.

'Are you okay?' he asked.

'I'm good. It's you I'm worried about. You look exhausted.'

Filming wasn't quite finished. There were a few small scenes and some retakes left, but the hardest parts were over.

Then there was the premiere of *Sanctuary*. And then…back to LA. But LA without Gracie, that was difficult to imagine. Bed without Gracie was impossible.

Eating breakfast, going to sleep…everything without Gracie.

He was due back in the States soon to promote a movie he'd shot last summer. He had commitments that couldn't be moved.

Maybe he could convince her to take some leave from her job and come with him. To see the world. To experience more than just her cottage and the four walls of the White Horses Swim School.

It wasn't such an outrageous idea. There were swimming schools everywhere. She'd have no problem finding a job. Gracie wouldn't be content unless she was working, and he didn't expect her to give that up.

Besides, there were her parents. And the fact that she had ended her engagement because she couldn't leave them.

*You think that because you're a famous star, Gracie will make an exception and upend her entire life for you?*

No. He didn't think that. He knew her too well. The trappings of fame and celebrity were a liability, not an enticement. Why would anyone, let alone Gracie, give up their normal life for him?

'You were amazing,' she said.

He nodded and rested his head against her shoulder, unable to speak.

# CHAPTER TEN

Connor was half asleep before they'd even arrived home. He stumbled inside, went to his room and collapsed on his bed. 'I'll be out in a minute,' he muttered, but she told him to sleep.

She watched him from the doorway as Biscuit meowed and circled her legs.

He was amazing. Not that there'd been much doubt, but after watching him perform today, Gracie's regard for him had increased exponentially.

No one else would know what an achievement today had been for him. Oh, they'd watch the scene and be moved by it, but knowing that just a few weeks ago he couldn't swim a stroke made what he'd done today even more remarkable.

'If only you could let the world know. If only Bruce and the studio weren't being so insistent about this,' she whispered.

Gracie heated up dinner for herself and ate it by the pool, watching the lights twinkling on the harbour. She loved this view. She loved the water. She laughed softly to herself. It was strange, her complicated relationship with water, loving the very thing that had taken her sister from her.

Her mind raced, but her legs were too tired to move, so she sat out there for ages, Biscuit on her lap. It was late when a noise inside the house startled her.

'Hey,' Connor said, rubbing his hair and walking out. 'What are you doing?'

'I couldn't sleep.'

'Yeah, I had the opposite problem.'

'You were shattered. I'm not surprised after the day you had. Are you hungry?'

'Yes, I think I am.'

'Leanne left us a chicken curry and rice. I'm not hungry, but do you want some?'

Gracie made to stand, but Connor waved her down. 'I'll get it.'

He came back the patio a while later with dinner for himself and wine for both of them.

'Tell me honestly, Gracie, are you okay after today?'

'I'm absolutely fine. It was upsetting at first, but as the day went on, I think I figured some things out.'

'Like what?'

'Like how so many factors conspire to make anything happen. How things can go from good to bad in an instant. And the reverse.' It had given her a different perspective on the world. 'And I've also been thinking about how amazing you are.'

'You don't have to say that.'

'Yes, I absolutely do, because I'm the only one who knows exactly what you did today.' *And I'm the only one who will ever know because of your stupid contract.* 'You didn't just give a moving performance, Connor. You did it over and over, and… and you did it while in the water. Something you couldn't have done a few weeks ago.'

'Thanks to you.'

'No. *You* did it. It was all you.'

He shook his head. 'I couldn't have done it without you.'

'You could,' she insisted.

'I couldn't.'

'Are we seriously having an argument about this?' She laughed, and he smiled.

Connor ate, and she sipped her wine and thought again how perfect this moment was. How she wanted to capture it, bottle it, keep it forever. Instead she took out her phone and said, 'Smile,' and he did.

There. When it was over, she'd at least have that picture to look back on and remember that things could be perfect, if only for an evening.

He pushed his plate away and put his arm around her. They sat like that for a while longer, watching the harbour, which was now mostly dark, except for the occasional light blinking on the opposite shore.

'We should get to bed, don't you think?' she

asked, but Connor answered her with a kiss. Soft and pleading, then hungry and hard. He reached under her shirt and she moaned, the desire inside her awoken and sparked.

'Gracie, for the record, you're the best kisser I know,' he said into her neck as he rubbed behind her ear with his nose.

'Well, I had a good teacher.'

She felt his laugh against her shoulder.

'But you didn't even finish telling me the rules.'

'I didn't?'

'You didn't get to rule ten.' She was sure of it. She'd been wondering ever since that night he'd lifted her onto his kitchen bench. 'What is rule ten? Of kissing?'

He squinted thoughtfully. 'Remind me of the other rules.'

She glared at him. 'I knew you were making them up!'

'I had to sound like I knew what I was doing.'

She laughed. 'Connor, I always believed you knew what you were doing.'

'So, since you've been such a good pupil, remind me again.'

'Rule one, don't chew your own lip.'

'A good rule in any circumstance.'

'Rule two, that should probably be rule one, make sure the other person consents.'

'Also a solid rule.'

'Pay attention to the other person, the position,

get close, don't be afraid to use your tongue. Close your eyes. Sound familiar?'

'Indeed.' Connor closed his eyes and leant into her.

'Rule ten? Tell me or I'll think you made them up,' she teased.

Connor blinked, then said, 'Rule ten is never to kiss alone. Always make sure there is someone else around.'

'You're copying that from the swim safety rules.' She pretended to swat him.

'So what? It's an excellent rule.' He moved in, and this time she conceded. He pressed his lips gently on the side of her mouth. Laid a trail of kisses along her chin, down her throat. But otherwise, he held himself back, only allowing his mouth to touch her, her collarbone, her shoulders, down her arm, to her hands. Each time she tried to pull him closer, he held back. The space between their bodies was driving her crazy. His slow progress was excruciating.

'I want you,' she pleaded.

'You have me. Gracie, you have me.'

And then they both gave in, and the evening that was already perfect became legendary.

Afterwards, they lay on the outdoor sofa, Connor on his back, Gracie sprawled on top of him, bodies limp.

'I don't want to move,' she said. 'Ever.'

He let out a long, low sigh. 'That's a shame, because I was going to ask you something.'

'What?'

'To come with me.'

'To bed?'

'No. To LA.'

Gracie froze and felt Connor still underneath her.

'You don't have to answer now. In fact, please don't answer now. I want you to think about it. Really, honestly think about whether you want to come with me. Not whether you think you should, or whether you think you can. But whether being with me is something, you, Gracie Sutherland, want to do.'

She pulled herself up from him. The combination of Connor's hard body and warm, enticing pheromones was too powerful not to cloud her judgement.

She couldn't possibly go to LA with him. And now she couldn't say no right away. She had to delay the inevitable.

'Why can't you stay here?' she asked.

'I have work there for the next month or so, but I could come back here after that,' he said.

Wow. She hadn't expected that answer.

'But my work is mostly based in LA. At least for the next few years.'

Years.

Gracie stood, and her knees almost gave way.

'I have to think.'

'Yes, definitely. I just wanted you to know what I was thinking. I wanted to be honest with you.'

They went to bed then. She was silent, but her thoughts were screaming.

LA was on the other side of the vast Pacific Ocean. Half a world away. It should seem impossible. Out of the question.

Yet as they lay entwined together, listening to the cicadas and the lapping waves, it felt impossible to say goodbye to Connor. To watch him get on a plane by himself. To stay here, to go back to her life as it had been, to the same three things: work, her parents and her own home.

That also seemed impossible.

The carpet really was red, and her dress was silver. Jenny had insisted that the colour complemented her pale skin and dark hair. Standing here, with everyone else made up to the nines, she was so grateful for Jenny's help. There was a short queue of people waiting to take their turn to walk along it for their photos. Bruce was there waiting for them.

'Red carpets are a bit silly,' Connor said. 'But it's for publicity. It's what's expected.'

'Of course. Should I wait for you at the other end?' she asked.

'No, you go with him,' Bruce said before Connor could answer.

At the look of horror on her face, Connor picked

up her hand and said, 'Just for a few pictures. For the ruse.'

Of course.

The ruse.

The story that they were in a relationship.

But weren't they really in a relationship? Last night he'd asked her to think about going to LA with him. She'd never felt so happy—or so terrified. Connor wanted to be with her. She'd thought this meant they were talking about something serious. Something permanent. Yet now he was saying *ruse* again? Was asking her to LA just about putting on a show for the cameras as well? Did he really want her to go with him, or was it just about keeping up the story that they were in a relationship? Was it just about keeping his secret? She had no time to question him, because she was being taken along to the carpet. They were up. The first camera flash made her startle, and Connor pulled her close. 'Are you okay with the lights?'

She nodded. Camera flashes were fine. 'I was just surprised.' *And worried and anxious and wondering why you just called our relationship a ruse for the first time in weeks.*

They stood and smiled and posed. A journalist called out, 'Connor! Gracie!'

To her eternal thanks, Bruce waved her over to him from the other end of the carpet. She wasn't going to need to answer any questions, and her blood pressure dropped instantly.

'Thanks.' She smiled at Bruce.

'Don't mention it. It's a lot, isn't it?'

She nodded, catching her breath.

'How are you doing? How are things with you and Connor?'

Gracie wasn't sure what he meant. There were four people who knew their relationship was a lie.

And only two who knew that lie was a farce. She wasn't going to complicate things by enlightening him.

'We're doing okay. Only a few days to go.'

'You aren't considering going back with him?'

Had Connor spoken to Bruce about his offer? Before they'd even agreed anything? Surely not. It was only last night, and Connor had asked her to think about it. Nothing was settled.

'My life is here. And…' *You know as well as I do that we're putting on a show for the cameras.*

'Just wondering.' Bruce shrugged.

Gracie wanted to like Bruce and trust him like Connor did, but something in the vagueness of his words, the way everything he said seemed heavy with innuendo, made it difficult. And then there was the fact that Bruce thought Connor needed to keep his swimming lessons a secret…

'It would be a big thing for me, to go with him.'

'Of course.'

'I don't know anything about his world. And I'm not sure, given what I do know, that I want to.'

This got Bruce's interest. He faced her and studied her for the first time.

'It seems so artificial. Contrived. *Fake*,' she added.

'Because we asked you to pretend to be in a relationship with him?'

'Yes, but it's more what caused that. The fact you and the studio wanted to lie about Connor's ability to swim.'

Bruce's brow creased. 'You know that was his idea, don't you?'

Gracie's face felt warm. The crowd, the bright lights made her skin flush.

'His idea?'

'I told him it would be great publicity if it was known that in addition to giving a great performance, he'd also had to learn to swim from scratch, but he was insistent it stay secret. Hence, you.'

'It was your idea and the studio's, not his,' Gracie said, as if that would make it so. She trusted Connor more than she trusted the word of this man she'd only met once. Didn't she?

'No, it was all Connor's idea. The studio didn't know anything about it. I helped him execute it. I didn't agree, but I love that man. There's nothing I wouldn't do for him.'

Connor was strolling towards them now, face beaming, duty done.

What should she do?

* * *

Gracie's eyes were wide, but her posture was tense. Bruce gave Connor an apologetic look and slipped away.

Something had happened. The cameras. Journalists. The crowd must have upset her.

'Is everything okay? Let's go in. It'll be quieter in there. Still lots of people but no cameras.'

She shook her head. 'Bruce is very grateful for everything I've done. *Everything.*'

She looked at him, straight into his soul, and he knew she knew.

'Gracie—'

'Did you lie to me?'

Denying it would be worse, but he wanted to hide the truth if only to save her from the hurt she was currently experiencing.

'I can explain. But let's go inside at least.'

She scoffed. 'It'd better be good. I'm not feeling particularly forgiving.'

The procession was stalling behind them. Guests were trying to move past them to get inside.

'Let's go somewhere more private. We can't talk here.'

But she didn't want to listen. 'Not knowing how to swim isn't shameful. You know exactly why I believe that. How could you? It was one thing to lie at the outset. But all your talk about how you could trust me. And that's why you were so evasive over being involved in raising money for our fund! How could you not tell me then? You lied to me.'

He tried to steer her into the theatre, aware that all eyes were on them. The cameras as well.

'We're holding everything up. People are noticing.'

She stood her ground. 'I'm not moving until you tell me the truth.'

'Gracie, please.' He leant in and muttered, 'I couldn't tell you because of my mother. I don't want her to know.'

She pulled a face, then shook her head. He tried again, but it was hard over the noise of the crowd and standing in their glare. Even if every camera wasn't pointed in their direction, it certainly felt like it.

'I lied to my mother that I could swim because I didn't want her to feel bad that she couldn't afford my lessons. I didn't want my brother to feel bad. My mom did everything she could to protect us from our father, and I didn't want to add to her stress.'

'But that was years ago.'

'I had to keep it going. I never wanted her to feel guilty about anything we had to do to survive. It would have hurt her, badly. And you know why I had to protect them.'

Connor caught Bruce's eye, who was already heading their way with Giselle, and the three of them finally got Gracie inside the theatre. They were away from the cameras, but there were still many people inside. And he couldn't trust any of them not to talk to an observant journalist.

'I can't trust you,' she whispered.

'Of course you can. I've told you the truth now.'

She shook her head, and for the first time, he noticed her eyes were glassy. His were rapidly threatening to go the same way. It wasn't unlike trying to save the boy in the ocean. Nothing he tried seemed to work, and Gracie was slipping further and further away from him. 'I don't think you've even been honest with yourself. I don't know what else you're keeping from me.'

They stood next to a pillar. Gracie faced him, but he faced the room. He could see the eyes that were pretending not to look at them. The ears that were turned their way.

'Nothing, Gracie, nothing at all.' This was the only thing he'd kept from her, and he needed her to see that. But he was losing her.

'I don't know what is real and what isn't,' she said.

'What's that supposed to mean?'

'I means exactly what I said. I'm not the one playing games.'

'I'm not playing games!'

'You just said this was all a ruse! You told me I had to smile for the cameras. To keep your secret.'

'I didn't mean… Gracie, I had to lie to protect my mother, that's all. She couldn't afford lessons.

You know what an awful time she had. I've told you everything about my father, my childhood. That was all the truth. I've been lying to her for years because I can't bear to upset her. I don't see what the big deal is.'

Gracie laughed, but it was so close to a cry, he wasn't even sure anymore. His eyes were losing the ability to focus.

'You lied to me, and you kept lying to me. Even when you told me about your father. It *is* a big deal.'

'I lied to protect my mother. You of all people should understand that. You've put your entire life on hold because you're worried about your parents. You'd do anything to look after them, and you know it.'

'So? They need me.'

'Do they? Really?'

'Yes.'

'But if you weren't here, they'd manage, wouldn't they?'

She closed her eyes and shook her head. 'It's not the same at all.'

'It is the same.'

She opened her eyes, wide and furious. 'Connor, you've just been telling me how you had to lie to me to protect your mother from a lie you've been telling for the last thirty years! Don't you dare lecture me about how I shouldn't care about my parents.'

*It's not...* he opened his mouth to say.

But it *was* the same thing. They were both obligated to their parents, tied by things that had happened decades ago. Things neither of them could change and neither could ever get past.

'You keep telling me I need to get over it, yet you're the one stuck in the past. I don't see you dealing with anything. Or do you think you don't need to? That since you're this successful, adored film star, different rules apply to you?'

He winced. That was a low blow.

She glared at his reaction. 'That's it, isn't it? *You're* allowed to have secrets, and *you* don't need to deal with your past, but *I* have to get over everything that happened with my sister.'

He wanted to argue, explain, and he tried to find the words. She felt a deep, enduring obligation to her parents, and that wasn't unlike his relationship with his own mother. He might be on the other side of the world from her right now, he might not even live in the same city, but that didn't make the bond they shared any less important than the one Gracie had with her parents. He still made decisions based on what had happened in his childhood. Based on his own feelings of guilt. His own fear of inadequacy. The determination he still felt that he needed to protect his family.

He knew what he'd done to Gracie was unforgiveable. So when Gracie said, 'I'm leaving,' there was no point stopping her.

'It's over. All of it. Every single relationship we have. The fake, the real. And the professional. Over.'

He couldn't stop her. Or the cameras. Or the chatter around them.

It was over.

He'd made a lot of mistakes in his life. But the way he'd handled this situation with Gracie had been by far the worst.

His relationship with Gracie was the one thing he'd never be able to save.

# CHAPTER ELEVEN

The banging on Gracie's door was louder and more insistent than the knocks she'd heard earlier that morning from a couple of presumptuous journalists. She wanted to shout to them to go away, but that would prove to whoever was waiting outside that she really was home. Her curtains were closed, and she'd resolved not to leave her house until everyone had left. She hadn't answered the numerous calls or messages from Virginia or her parents. And especially not the calls from Connor.

They would all be furious at her. And she didn't care. Not one little bit.

Connor had lied to her.

And then he'd had the nerve to say that she should understand why he'd lied, because she knew what it was like to want to protect your parents. Each time she remembered his words, she recoiled. What he had done and the situation with her parents were two totally different things. Connor had lied. To the whole world, but most of all to Gracie. She was only doing her best to care for her parents, who needed her.

Totally different things.

What a nerve.

The knocking continued.

'Gracie. It's us. Open up.'

What were her parents doing here? It was a zoo outside! She didn't want to see them, but she couldn't leave them out there either. She stood with her ear against her door, listening, waiting, hoping they would give up and leave, but when her mother knocked and called again, Gracie relented. She shielded her face and quickly let her parents in.

'What are you thinking! They'll have taken so many of photos of you!'

'We don't care. We needed to see if you were okay. You aren't answering anyone's calls.'

'Of course I'm not.'

She walked back down her hallway to her living room. The furthest room away from the front door, but still not far enough.

'Everyone's saying you and Connor broke up,' Sharon began.

'We did.'

Her parents still didn't know about the pretend relationship, and at this point, there didn't seem any point telling them. It wouldn't achieve anything except more recriminations.

*Dating a Hollywood star was a very bad idea. You were always bound to get your heart broken and the remains of it picked over by the entire world.*

'They're also saying you broke up with him. Is that right?'

She nodded. Yes. She had ended it. But that didn't mean her heart wasn't currently in a million tiny little pieces smeared across the phone screens of the world. 'It was bound to happen eventually.' She shrugged.

'But why?' her father asked.

'Because…lots of reasons.' *He's a serial liar.* 'Apart from anything else, I'm not going to leave the pair of you.' She smiled. Stepped towards her mother for a hug. They had to see that her being with Connor was a very bad idea.

But her mother held a hand up. 'Why can't you leave us?'

'Because you need me.'

Her mother and father exchanged a look. 'I sincerely hope that's not the reason you broke up,' he said.

She shook her head. Was it? No, she'd walked out last night because Connor hadn't been truthful. And because he'd been cruel with his remarks about her parents.

So many factors.

'Gracie, is it possible that *you* need *us*?'

'Of course, but…no. It isn't just the distance. It's everything. Perhaps you've heard he's a famous actor? Very good-looking, immensely talented. And did I mention famous?'

'So it's his fame that worries you?' Sharon sat,

and her father went to the kitchen and filled the kettle.

Gracie sat too.

That was the thing. Connor's fame didn't worry her. At first, maybe, it had been strange, but now she knew the real Connor. Now she knew that the media attention was not a part of him.

*You know the real Connor.*

No, she didn't.

The real reason she'd stormed out was that he hadn't been truthful. She couldn't trust him.

*He had a reason for lying. He told you about his mother. He told you everything except that it was his idea to keep the lessons a secret. He still showed you parts of himself he hasn't shown other people.*

She shook her head. 'We just have very different lives.'

She hoped the inquisition was over and waited while her father made them all tea. She accepted a mug gratefully and wrapped her hands around it.

'Well, was it at least fun while it lasted?' he asked.

Despite herself, Gracie smiled. Her parents saw the look of happiness flash across her face, so there was no point denying it.

She sighed. 'It doesn't matter if I did or not. He lied to me.'

'About something important?'

'Yes.' It was very important. It was the basis of everything. 'He lied about being able to swim.'

The way her parents frowned told her they were confused. Of course they were.

'Sorry, I wasn't meant to tell you that. Please, please don't ask me anything else. Virginia could be in a lot of trouble if it gets out.'

Her father leant forward. 'We don't actually know what you're talking about, so we won't say anything. But Gracie, has this all got anything to do with Caroline?'

'No.'

He looked unconvinced. 'Really?'

'Doesn't everything in our lives come back to her?' Gracie asked.

Her father picked up her mother's hand. 'Losing Caroline was the worst thing that ever happened to us. And it always will be. We will never get over it. And nor will you. But that doesn't mean we have to put our lives on hold. We keep going, the best that we can.'

'She would have wanted you to live the best, most wonderful, and fullest life you possibly can,' her mother added.

Gracie shook her head. 'It was my fault she died. It's not that easy for me to do that.'

'It wasn't your fault!' her father exclaimed.

'It was. I snuck out for a swim. You said we couldn't, and I went anyway. It's my fault she followed me.'

'We're your parents. We should have been paying more attention. Besides, there were other people at the pool. Other adults who didn't react in time. Paramedics who were delayed by another accident. A lifesaver who should have been on duty but wasn't. It was never your fault. You were only a child,' her father insisted firmly.

'You weren't responsible for her then, and you aren't responsible for us now,' Sharon added.

Her parents' words reminded her of watching the filming of Connor's big scene, saving his on-screen son. Of how the scene had played out in so many different ways. How tragedy could turn to elation in a heartbeat. And vice versa.

How precarious life was.

But also how precious.

Her parents didn't blame her. They never had, but it would take her a long time to get her head around that. And even longer for her heart to accept it.

When her parents left, Gracie messaged Virginia to let her know she was still alive.

Are they angry about the deal? Do they want their money back? she asked. Better to find out and face the music.

Virginia called Gracie right away.

'I haven't heard a peep from them.'

'Not at all? Not even Bruce?'

'Nope. And the last instalment went into my

account this morning. It looks like we're getting the pools fixed.'

'They paid?' Gracie was incredulous.

'Seems so. Do you want to talk about it?'

Gracie shook her head even though it was just an audio call. 'I'll be back at work tomorrow.'

'Take your time, please.'

'I'll be there.' Gracie hung up.

Connor had paid. For the lessons. For her dubious acting ability. The deal was done.

This should have been an enormous relief. Even if Connor and Bruce were angry with her for storming out of the premiere, they hadn't reneged on the original deal. White Horses would get its new pool.

And yet it also meant that Gracie would never see or hear from Connor ever again.

The following morning, Gracie was giving Biscuit her breakfast when her phone buzzed with a message from Virginia. It was a link to a newspaper article.

*Connor Day: How I learned to swim*

*Gracie Sutherland of White Horses Swim School is more than just Connor Day's new love: She also taught him to swim.*

Gracie yelped and nearly dropped her phone.

*When Connor Day found he was expected to swim for his new role in Gerry Johns's new movie, he panicked. Luckily the perfect teacher was only a phone call away.*

*Gracie Sutherland is a swim instructor at White Horses Swim School, where she teaches people of all ages—from six months to ninety-six—how to swim.*

*Connor told us, 'Not being able to swim is nothing to be ashamed of. Many people can't or don't learn for reasons beyond their control. In my case, it was because my family lacked the means. And once I could afford it, I was too ashamed to admit that I had never learnt.'*

*The movie is being filmed in Sydney and stars Connor Day and Giselle Boucher as a couple struggling in the aftermath of the drowning of a child.*

*'We've nearly wrapped up filming,' said Johns. 'The film is due for release next year. I'm very excited for you all to see it. Giselle and Connor have given Oscar-worthy performances, and everyone who has been involved has told me how moving they have found it.'*

*'Water is dangerous, and knowing how to swim could save your life or someone else's,' Connor added. 'Not being able to swim is nothing to be embarrassed or ashamed about, and if I can learn at thirty-five, anyone can.'*

*The producers, Grand Ecran Productions, will be donating a percentage of the profits of the new movie to a charity to support swimming lessons for disadvantaged children...*

Now Gracie really did drop her phone. She had to find Connor before he left the country.

Gracie rushed out her front door, still wearing her yellow rashie and black shorts. There was no time to change. What if he'd left already? She had no idea what she was going to say to him or even if he wanted to see her, but...she had to try.

Reversing out of the driveway and onto the street, she heard tyres squeal and felt a bump. Her car rocked back and forth, and so did she.

She'd been hit. It hadn't been a huge bump. Neither car had been going fast.

She glanced in her rearview mirror.

*You have got to be kidding me.*

She rested her arms and head on the steering wheel, not yet ready for this conversation. Moments later, Connor was knocking on her window.

'Are you alright? I'm so sorry.'

She got out of her car. Her hands tingled, though whether that was from the shock of the accident or from seeing Connor, she wasn't sure.

'It was my fault,' she said.

'No, it was mine. I wasn't paying attention.'

'I was reversing into the road. It was my fault.'

'Are we really arguing about this?' Connor asked. Then his face broke into a smile, and she laughed. The sort of laugh that comes from shock and the release of stress, a strangled high-pitched cry.

'Are you really alright?' Connor leant towards her and touched her arm gently.

'I'm okay. You?'

'Fine. I am truly sorry. I was distracted.'

'Me too,' she admitted. She'd been concentrating on getting back to Watsons Bay before he left and really hadn't looked properly. Thank goodness it was Connor pulling up and not another car travelling at speed.

'Where are you off to?' he asked.

'To find you.'

'Me?'

'Yes, you! To catch you before you leave. What are you doing here?'

'I came to see you. I came to say goodbye.'

Right. Goodbye. Of course.

Connor nodded in the direction of the single remaining paparazzo, who looked ecstatic, and she gestured towards her front door.

Biscuit was happy to see Connor and meowed and rubbed herself against his legs. Gracie closed her front door but didn't move further down her hallway.

He'd come to say goodbye.

'What time's your flight?'

'Later today, but…'

'Right, then I guess this is…goodbye.'

*It's all over. He's really leaving. Without me.*

She shifted her weight from foot to foot. 'You didn't have to tell the world you couldn't swim,' she said.

'I did. You were right. I shouldn't have insisted it be kept secret in the first place. I shouldn't have felt ashamed.'

'Connor, I don't think you were ashamed. I think you were trying to protect the people you loved, your mother, your brother.'

'That's what I told myself.'

'It wasn't true?'

'No. I mean yes. Gracie, I want to be completely honest with you. I should have told *you* the truth. You of all people.'

'What is the truth?' It felt as though the bottom was falling out of her world. She'd been trying to accept that he'd had good reasons for lying to her. She had almost convinced herself that he did.

'I was worried that… I wasn't enough. That there was something wrong with me. That I wasn't really a good actor. That I was a lucky fake. I was worried about telling people the truth. I thought I had to hide everything that wasn't perfect about myself.'

He paused, holding his breath. She nodded.

'I was scared I was too much like my father, getting by on my looks and charm. And worst of all, manipulating the truth. I lied to so many people. Not just my mother, but I lied to the world. I told the world I had a normal childhood. I couldn't ever tell the truth. I was always spinning a story.'

Her heart cracked open a little more. She thought of young Connor, hiding from his father. Helping to hide his mother and brother.

She wanted to reach for him. To touch him, to hold him, and it took every ounce of restraint she possessed to not to reach out.

'You're nothing like your father. You never have been.'

'That doesn't stop me worrying that I might be. But I have to start doing that. I have to start being honest with the people I love.'

He stood before her, face open. Did he mean her? No, he was talking about his mother.

'Have you spoken to your mum?'

'Several times. She's furious with me.'

'Because you didn't tell her you couldn't swim?'

'Yes, but mostly that I made you lie for me.'

Gracie shook her head.

'You told me on the very first day we met that it was nothing to be ashamed about,' Connor said.

'I still do believe that, but it's possible I was also overly judgemental.'

'No, you weren't. You were right.'

'I was struggling with my own issues.'

'Which are legitimate and real, and I shouldn't have said what I said to you the other night.'

One by one, her worries began to fall away, and her body felt looser, lighter. Even if Connor was leaving, it was a relief to say all of this out loud.

'You weren't wrong. I've been caught in my past as well. I was holding back, pushing people away. I've let guilt dictate my life for way too long. I'm going to try to find a way to change.'

'No, don't change. Not ever. You're perfect.' He shook his head and smiled again. The famous Connor Day smile. Even more brilliant at close range.

It felt like a goodbye, and yet he wasn't leaving.

'What happens now?' she asked slowly.

'That depends on you.'

'Me?'

'On whether you've thought about my offer. Whether you want to come with me.'

An ember of hope that had almost been extinguished now began to burn again.

'You still want me to come with you?'

'More than ever.'

'Just so we're clear, you want me to move with you to LA?'

He nodded.

The shocks of the past five minutes caught up with her in a rush. Reading the interview with Connor, crashing into him with her car. And now this.

She sobbed. A loud, harsh sob. Helpless to hold it back. Connor wrapped her instantly in a tight hug.

'No, Gracie, no. Are you sure you're alright?'

She nodded, caught her breath in several loud rasping gulps.

'Really? You still want me to come? After I stormed out of the premiere?'

'So? I'm the one who's sorry. I'm the one who messed up. I'm the one who wasn't honest. Gracie, please come with me. I don't want to swim alone in my pool. You should see it. It has a view over one of the canyons. Not quite as impressive as Sydney Harbour, but spectacular nonetheless.'

Her sobs turned into laughter, and this time he stopped them with a kiss. As his lips touched hers, her heart pounded in deep, even beats, and she felt more secure than she had in days, supported in his arms.

When he pulled back and looked her in the eye, he said, 'And in the interest of being completely open and honest with each other, I think I should tell you that I love you.'

There was a pause, long enough for Gracie's heart to start beating again and for Connor's expression to change from hope to concern before she said, 'I love you too.' She didn't need to think, didn't need to worry and didn't need to doubt.

He hugged her again. It was like a dream; impractical, impossible. Unreal.

'Wait, wait, how will it work? Will I live with you? What will I do? What about my parents?'

'We can go wherever you want. I can work around things. If you need to be here, we'll figure that out too. I want to be with you. The where isn't as important as being with you.'

She nodded. She didn't want Connor to give up his work, and she was starting to think that she needed a change in direction.

'We'll figure it all out together. We can do it. We'll just follow the rules.'

She rolled her eyes. 'Connor, I'm being serious.'

'So am I. Do you remember the rules of kissing?'

'No biting your own lips, don't be afraid to use your tongue. Listen to what the other person is telling you. How does that help?'

'What's rule ten of swimming and kissing?'

'Don't do it alone,' she said, smiling.

'You'll never have to,' he said, and kissed her.

# EPILOGUE

'I'M LOOKING FORWARD to meeting you tomorrow, as well. It's an honour to be working with you.' Gracie ended her phone call to the CEO of SwimSafe, one of the US's largest swimming charities, and looked around the airport for Connor.

'Sorry, I had to take that,' she said to him.

'Of course. My girlfriend, the high-flying executive.' He pulled her into a hug.

'Ha-ha.'

'It's true. I'm so proud of you.'

Six months after storming away from Connor at the film premiere, Gracie had found herself setting up a multimillion-dollar charity with the money the studio, Connor and his co-stars had donated from their fees from the film. The charity was just getting off the ground, but it would fund swimming lessons for children across the world. In addition to the money Connor and his co-stars and the film studio had pledged, other donations continued to flow in. Gracie had been on a steep learning curve, but Thibault had put her in touch with accountants and lawyers who were helping her.

She also now had several commitments to meet with the boards of related organisations to speak about her experiences and the importance of water safety. Talking to people she had never in a million years imagined speaking to. Uncomfortable at first, she soon realised how easy she found it to speak to people, even strangers, about something she was so passionate about.

She was doing things she never thought she would. Going to places she never dreamed of going.

Including Boston, Massachusetts, to meet Connor's family.

If her new role as CEO of the charity was not enough of a whirlwind, her relationship with Connor was like a cyclone.

A week after what they called 'the car crash', Gracie had taken Biscuit and a big leap and got on a plane to LA. Virginia had promised she would always have a job with her if things didn't work out, but six months in, Gracie couldn't imagine going back.

She spoke to her parents every other day, and they were doing well without her. If not thriving. They had been making new friends and community connections, and Gracie realised they wouldn't have done this while she had been there to be their constant sounding board. They had also visited Gracie and Connor in LA.

As for where they would live in the future, that

was still up in the air. Which was fine. They had the rest of their lives to figure things out.

And now they were landing at Logan Airport to meet Connor's family.

The northeast was cooler than Los Angeles, but the greeting they received was warm. His mother, brother, sister-in-law, and nieces were all at the gate to greet them.

'You didn't need to come. I told you we could have got a ride,' Connor said.

'You'll never be so famous that your mother won't pick you up from the airport,' Sinead said, eyes glistening as she hugged her son.

Connor wore a Red Sox cap and dark glasses and would have been unrecognisable to most people, though Gracie could always sense when he was near.

'Besides, we're not here for you anyway. We're here for Gracie,' Yumi said, pulling her into a big hug.

Connor and Callum fought over who would push the luggage trolley, and Sinead kept her arm tightly around Gracie as they walked to the car, everyone speaking at once.

It was remarkable how this was the first time she was seeing his family in person, yet they already felt like her own.

'What a story you both have,' said Sinead. 'I want to hear all of it. And the truth this time.'

'Not my smoothest effort,' Connor said with an abashed smile.

'Maybe not, but love rarely goes smoothly. I'm just glad you two found each other.'

*You hardly know me*, Gracie thought.

As if reading her mind, Sinead added, 'The woman who convinced Connor to finally open up must be a very special woman.'

Connor slid his own arm back around Gracie. 'That she is.'

Gracie pulled in close to Connor. As she did so, she felt again the cool chain around her neck carrying the ring Connor had given her the night before. Gracie had been sitting by Connor's pool, the one he'd never been able to swim in previously. Connor had just got out of it and had sat next to her in nothing but his swimming shorts. Seemingly from nowhere, he'd produced a small box and opened it to reveal a gorgeous ring set with a sapphire the colour of the ocean.

'This has been burning a hole in my pocket for weeks. I've been trying to find the perfect moment, but then I realised that every moment we spend together is perfect. Gracie, will you marry me?'

Surprised, she had tearfully accepted without hesitation.

She loved the way the ring looked on her finger, couldn't get used to the feeling of it, but until they told their families, the ring was a secret and safely pressed against her chest. The ring was beautiful, but what it symbolised meant so much more. The love and commitment of a wonderful man, her best friend. Her closest confidant. The man she trusted more than any other.

As if sensing her thoughts, Connor whispered to her, 'I can't wait to tell them.'

'Me neither.'

'What are you whispering about?' Naomi asked.

'I'm just checking Gracie isn't overwhelmed by all your attention.'

'She's fine,' Yumi said. 'She knows we love her.'

Gracie must have looked as dumbfounded as she felt. She'd only met Connor's family in person a few minutes ago. Everything that had happened to her over the past while had been amazing, and the old Gracie would have found it too much, but she didn't feel overwhelmed. Apart from anything, she had Connor. And always would. She hugged him tight, and he squeezed her back.

* * * * *

*If you enjoyed this story, check out these other great reads from Justine Lewis*

CEO's Spanish Fling
Italian Tycoon to Remember
Dating Game with Her Enemy
How to Win Back a Royal

*All available now!*

# Get up to 4 Free Books!

## We'll send you 2 free books from each series you try
## PLUS a free Mystery Gift.

Both the **Harlequin®** Historical and **Harlequin®** Romance series feature compelling novels filled with emotion and simmering romance.

**YES!** Please send me 2 FREE novels from the Harlequin Historical or Harlequin Romance series and my FREE Mystery Gift (gift is worth about $10 retail). I may cancel anytime by emailing ReaderServiceInfo@Harlequin.com or by calling 1-800-873-8635. If I don't cancel, I will receive 5 new Harlequin Historical books every month and be billed just $6.39 each in the U.S. or $7.19 each in Canada, or 4 new Harlequin Romance Larger-Print books every month and be billed just $7.19 each in the U.S. or $7.99 each in Canada, a savings of 20% off the cover price. It's quite a bargain! Shipping and handling is just 75¢ per book in the U.S. and $1.75 per book in Canada.* I understand that accepting the free books and gift places me under no obligation to buy anything—they are mine to keep for free no matter what I decide.

Choose one:
☐ Harlequin Historical (246/349 BPA G3CD)
☐ Harlequin Romance Larger-Print (119/319 BPA G3CD)
☐ Or Try Both! (246/349 & 119/319 BPA G3CE)

Name (please print)

Address     Apt. #

City     State/Province     Zip/Postal Code

**Email:** Please check this box ☐ if you would like to receive newsletters and promotional emails from Harlequin Enterprises ULC and its affiliates. You can unsubscribe anytime.

### Mail to the Harlequin Reader Service:
**IN U.S.A.:** P.O. Box 1341, Buffalo, NY 14240-8531
**IN CANADA:** P.O. Box 603, Fort Erie, Ontario L2A 5X3

Want to explore our other series or interested in ebooks? Visit www.ReaderService.com or call 1-800-873-8635.



HHHRLP2603